When Tayler is sent to Beta City to help its citizens disconnect from the all-knowing Social Media Central, he becomes the target of a deadly game.

Augmented reality players wearing head to toe gaming suits believe he is the Enemy Alien, and they shoot to kill. So Tayler is forced to hide in a secret bunker, trapped, with no way to escape this urban nightmare.

And as his friends hatch a plan to get him back home, they find the person toying with Tayler's life is more AI than human.

VIRTUAL INSANITY

TAYLER, BOOK TWO

KEVIN KLEHR

A NineStar Press Publication

www.ninestarpress.com

Virtual Insanity

First Edition, August 2022

ISBN: 978-1-64890-536-0

Also available in eBook, ISBN: 978-1-64890-535-3

CONTENT WARNING:
This book contains sexual content, which may only be suit-able for mature readers. Depictions of abduction, torture, death of a prominent character, and animal death.

To my husband, Warren, for your constant love and support.

To Clinton, for your passionate ideas.

To Mary, for being a fan.

To Angus, for helping me with that initial spark.

And to fellow writers, Rebecca Langham, M.D. Neu, J.P. Jackson, Glenn Quigley, Eric David Roman, and Christian Baines. Sharing our fears and our triumphs strengthens us all.

CHAPTER ONE

I HEARD A song from the 1960s. An American singer asserted "we're talking but we're not communicating". Someone played it on a radio stream while I've been here at Cradle Edge, and it got me thinking.

For the last month, I've been meeting people simply to get to know them. Getting to know what makes them tick. What their quirks are. How they use their charm to make me part of their circle.

And as they got to know me better, they shared their opinions while remaining open to being challenged. Plus, by this stage, I understood why they thought the way they did because I knew their backstories.

This wasn't the case back home in Astra City. Opinions were first and foremost linked to someone's brand, thanks to Social Media Central. We knew avatars or profile pics but never met the person. Never drank with them, laughed with them, or shared mutual stories. And even if we spoke through a video hook-up, it was always for less time than I spent with someone here in the bars at Cradle Edge.

Okay, to be fair, I was doing the same thing with the Social Media Socialites, my small friendship network back home. But I was one of the chosen few.

At the same time, I was navigating two relationships and losing myself in the process. Madeline Q, or Madi, as she liked to be known, was very persuasive. Every time I wasn't sure who I wanted to stay the night with, the sun was coming up before I knew it and she was waking in my arms.

Mike brought out my wild side more than Madi. My carnal desires overrode my cautious temperament when I was with him. He led me down paths I never imagined I'd delight in. It was not that Madi wasn't wild. She provided the equilibrium from my *boys being boys* sessions with Mike. I liked the balance in the bedroom I was getting between these two individuals.

So here I was four weeks without them, learning to love the most important person I'd discovered—me. And although it's nice to be desired, it's nice to *hear* yourself. I was arising from a state of mind that was controlled from the outside. Bombarded by the cyber world.

Cradle Edge was a small town of open fields and brick buildings. Nothing like the steel and glass jungle of my home. I needed this time away.

They have these things in everyone's homes called phones. They're like a device without screens. They come in all shapes and sizes. Some are novelties, as in the shape of a cartoon animal. Some stand upright while some are low set and bulky. You can contact anyone here if you know their "number". A number is a set of six or so digits that makes someone else's phone ring. And if you don't know their number you can press three numbers that let you talk to an "operator". The operator can look up anyone and connect you.

There are also "phone booths" on various streets where you can go if you need to contact someone when you're not home. What's really cool about this is you get a sense of anonymity when you're out and about. No one knows where you are. It's a really odd yet addictive feeling.

And there were shops! Stores I'd never seen in Astra City. People liked giving ornaments as gifts, as many homes were full of knickknacks that told you a lot about who lived there. And people regularly groomed. They got haircuts and made new clothes. Back home, folk were only getting used to the idea of dressing to be noticed. Too many years acting anonymous behind a screen robbed many of developing a sense of style. A sense of self.

Now I fully understood me, and I'm no puppet for anyone's algorithm.

IT WAS ANOTHER upbeat night as I waited for Carter at the Unicorn Hotel, a pub in the artists' hub of Cradle Edge. I was engaged in conversation about what clothes say about an era, listening mostly, as it wasn't a topic I knew much about. Frederica, a student of fashion, and her bearded friend Ralph were trying to pinpoint when design ended and comfort took over. They complimented me on the sci-fi design on my T-shirt, which led to this discussion. I grinned, interjected a little, then grinned some more, dying for Carter to get here.

"But what about the era of the tight T-shirt?" Ralph was questioning Frederica.

"Everything was *tight* back in the 1970s," she replied. "And nearly a hundred years on, people are constricting themselves again." She gestured to the other patrons.

Frederica was right. A trend had caught on. Several, who had good bodies to show off, were hugged by their nap-shirts. A design based on what patients with severe mental illness used to be bound in during the twentieth century. The only difference, these garments allowed you to move your arms. Not many people knew what they were wearing had a dark past. They thought the wraparound belts in contrasting colours were the height of fashion. But as I already mentioned, trends caught on more here than they did in Astra City. People saw each other out and about and made decisions on what was in and what was out.

A topless man with tattoos caught my eye. He was a refreshing antidote to the sea of nap-shirts. He was toasting to something-or-other with his mates, as the bartender piled their drinks on the counter. Nearby, a small group danced to a tune no one else could hear. Their rhythm was infectious as a male couple mirrored their moves. And three spirited friends finessed the art of hand gestures as they debated. Four weeks on and this sense of connection still made me smile.

"What do you think of these nap-shirts, Tayler?" Frederica asked me.

"I like them, but I wouldn't wear one."

"Why not?"

I studied the garment in question once more.

"I don't know. I *want* to be daring in my fashion choices, but it's not something I'd wear." An alluring woman with straight blonde hair sported one in stark mustard and black. "Maybe that's my problem. I'm trapped in my own conventions."

"Or maybe you know your own style," said Ralph.

"Fashion was invented for those without a sense of style," Frederica added.

Ralph smirked. "Speaking of style—"

"Oh, you're going to bring this up again." Frederica crossed her arms.

"Bring up what?" I asked.

"My black suit with frilly sleeves."

"Oh, that outfit."

"Hey! It's a Frederica original."

"A Frederica original what?" Ralph's smirk got wider.

"A Frederica original disaster," I replied.

She slapped me playfully on the cheek.

"I wore it the night Carter introduced me to Tayler."

"And you wore *that* for a first impression?" Ralph glanced my way.

"It made an impression." I raised my champagne glass. "An impression of a very *unique* lady."

"I want to challenge you." Frederica gazed at me. "I want to see you in a nap-shirt." She clinked her glass with mine. "The next time we meet, you're wearing a nap-shirt!"

"I accept the challenge." I looked down at my chest, trying to imagine my torso strapped with buckles. "Yeah, I'll give it a try."

Ralph looked at his watch. "It's not like Carter to be late."

I first met Carter and his friend Hendrix in Astra City. They both hailed from Cradle Edge, which is the reason why I chose this place to take a break. I met them when they called themselves the Life Experience Mob. They helped the citizens of Astra City reconnect with history by simulating forgotten experiences like school and Christmas. They'd gained an education here in Cradle Edge. I only went to school until I was twelve in Astra City. After that, all our education moved online.

Frederica and I glanced at the clock above the wide assortment of decorative liquor bottles.

"You're right," she said. "Carter's never late."

Like an actor timing his cue, Carter entered the bar. He was frazzled.

"What's wrong?" I asked.

He half smiled at each of us. We smiled back.

"I have a favour to ask, Tayler. But I just got here. I don't want to burst in on your conversation. What were you talking about before I interrupted?"

"How you're never late," Frederica replied.

"Ha-ha. No, seriously, what were you talking about?"

"That's what we were talking about," Ralph replied.

"So why are you late?" Frederica asked.

"Hmm." Carter sighed. "I had a visitor just as I was leaving to meet you. It seems Beta City needs my help."

We all shared glances as if clarity could be found in one another's expressions.

"Continue," I said.

"Tayler, I want you to go to Beta City. Check it out for a few days. It seems they're just as lost as Astra City was. Worse even. Social Media Central has been ramped up a notch. No one is communicating with each other at all." Carter smirked, as if to play down how fanatical he sounded. "I'll meet you after I finish some business here." He glanced at the others. "Am I being a killjoy? This can't be as interesting as talking about a million other things."

"You've got us intrigued," Frederica replied. "What's Tayler supposed to do when you meet up?"

"We're going to find people to help us create a team. Beta City needs the Life Experience Mob."

"Why don't you ask Hendrix to help you?" I asked.

"This is *his* idea. He's the one who just came and saw me. He was in Beta City and said they're like zombies there."

"And so why doesn't *he* help you?" I repeated.

"He can't. Special project." Carter placed his finger to his lips. "And I have something to attend to before we begin." He shook his head. "Sorry, Tayler. I sound like a spy caught between missions. It was his suggestion to have you on my team. You know what it's like to live in a society where no one connects. Reality is a construct." He grinned. "You know what it's like when everyone around you is addicted to Social Media Central."

I was oddly empowered.

"That's the look of someone with a calling." Ralph winked at me.

"How brain-dead are they in Beta City?" I asked.

"They're not exactly brain-dead," Carter said.

"Not brain-dead? You made it sound like their lives are as complex as a pillow," Ralph argued.

"No. A new trend has got them. Actually, the more I think about it, I guess they are brain-dead. They're zombies to this new craze."

"And everyone's addicted?" I asked.

"Not everyone. But this extension of Social Media Central has wide-reaching implications. People will get hurt. That's why we need to bring reality back to them."

"This conversation is morbid." Frederica scrunched her lips. "All you boys seem to do is save people with stunted social skills. If they want to plug into Social Media Central and tune out of the real world, so be it. Let them. It's *their* lives."

"You know, studies show that people hooked on SMC don't live long," said Ralph.

"Yeah, and they eat badly and only have cybersex," Frederica added. "And they trap all their emotions inside, never dealing with them. We've all read the studies."

"But that's just it," Carter said. "People on Social Media Central don't see that research. And even if they did, they wouldn't know how to reconnect. They'd sit in a room of other addicts and struggle to have a conversation."

He crossed his arms and exhaled. I suspected once again he was concerned about sounding more obsessive than passionate.

Frederica placed her hand on his shoulder. "So, let them burn in binary-code hell." She shook her head like a mother giving up on her drug-addicted child. "It's not your problem, Carter. Yours neither, Tayler. Beta City is full of rejects, and they got themselves there. No one forced them."

Although she made sense, my gut was telling me otherwise. My instincts craved new challenges. *Save Beta City?*

Why not! My belief in humanity had been restored here. I enjoyed nuances in speech patterns where words could take on new meaning, not be misinterpreted in a written comment. And smiling seemed cooler. People wore real *I'm in love with life* smiles. Like they'd started to in Astra City. Like they should in Beta City.

It was time to finish my holiday and go on an adventure.

"When can you leave?" Carter asked me.

"What do I do when I get there?"

He reached into his jeans and pulled out his wallet. He dropped a wad of cash, held in place with an elastic band, next to my champagne glass.

"Meet people. Get a feel for the place. Get laid a hundred times for all I care. But don't use credit cards. Stay untraceable. Just make sure you meet me in three days."

"Where?"

He unravelled the money, showing me a strip of paper inside. On it were details. I was to meet Carter on the red bench at Carrington Park at three o'clock.

"Now there's a challenge!" Frederica smirked.

"I thought you didn't care about Beta City," I said.

"I don't, Tayler. I don't give two raccoons about Beta City. But if you can get laid a hundred times in three days, that's a challenge worth considering."

CHAPTER TWO

NO CARTER. JUST a breeze blowing in search of the masses. But there were no masses. The trees were the only life form enjoying what the wind was offering. Except for me, of course. I sat on the red bench, frustrated that Carter was half an hour late. In this ghost town, there was no one to talk to, and I was desperate to talk to my friend. If I didn't use words soon, I'd be staring at my shoes and mumbling with a crazed expression.

Beta City was worse than Astra City had ever been. Everyone was their own prisoner, watching the world pass on Social Media Central, never letting their skin near natural light. From time to time, I'd see someone, or maybe a few people, covered in grey head-to-toe bodysuits that made them look like creepy mime artists. There was no way to tell who might be inside these snugly fitting costumes unless you had a good idea of the body shape of its wearer. Even the ears were tightly contoured which made me suspect these weird outfits were custom made for the individual.

These things had a bizarre face. The eyes, the nose, and the mouth were framed inside white plastic. But there was also fabric over the mouth so you could hear what the mystery human inside was saying. They communicated by shouting things that made no sense. I'd heard "Kill the blighter!", "He's a human dog", and "This would never be right in Sebastian's Lair" yelled at no one by these goons as they roamed the streets.

The day before, one of these individuals stopped behind me but acted as if I wasn't there. He, or she, had a miniature camera lens hidden above the glossy black Perspex covering the plastic eye shield. I'd worked for tech company, A.V. Enterprises, a long time ago, so I was used to seeing this type of camera. After standing like a robot whose battery was dead, this person screamed, "I can't take any more of your stray theories," then left.

Carter was now thirty-five minutes late. The surrealism of this place got to me. Three days prior, I'd arrived with just a backpack, searching for accommodation. And the anorexic lady who I was told to meet by one of Ralph's pals didn't even make eye contact with me. Her world consisted of nothing else but her device and Social Media Central. I finally found my room after swiping the card I was given in the lock of every unnumbered door.

This accommodation was luxurious, even if it felt lonely. Beta City was probably designed by wealthy architects who challenged each other to build the world's most sensational structures. Four such skyscrapers of varying height sat on an artificial harbour which shot out from the mainland like a beggar's hand reaching for coins.

Several treasures of this metropolis once existed in this precinct. A theatre, a concert hall, and a gallery had been transformed into apartment buildings. Their original signage had been restored, but their purpose belonged to a bygone era.

I was in a building that looked like a sheet of curved cardboard; one of three overlooking the harbour. They all shone, reflecting sunlight with their mirror finish. They stood tall above the highways that lay between them and the water. But no one took their cars on these roads. I doubt anyone knew how to drive.

Carter was now forty minutes late. The grey-clad trio had moved on. Hell, the grass had a more meaningful life than these weirdos.

Rainclouds were moving in. If Carter didn't make it soon, I'd need shelter. Or I'd need to go back and reclaim my accommodation.

"Tayler?" a funky woman with olive-toned skin asked.

"Yes."

"I'm Hudson."

Her hooped earrings, thin-framed glasses, and bold makeup choices made me wonder if she was from here. Her head was as bald as a bowling ball. And she smoked. Her vaping left a haze around her suspicious gaze.

"Carter couldn't make it, so he's sent me to meet you until he arrives."

"How long will he be?"

"He's not sure." She beckoned me. "Come." I stood.

"Who shaves your head?" I asked. It was an odd question but, as I never saw anything resembling a business district, let alone a hairdresser, it was the first thing that came to mind.

"I'm very good with a razor." She snickered. "No. A friend does this for me. Never any blood. Never any cuts. She slides the blade like she's spreading butter."

"You socialise?" I shook my head. "Dumb question. You're a friend of Carter's. You must socialise. Are you from Cradle Edge?"

"No. Those cyber-starved peeps are unrelatable."

"I like it there. I relate."

"I gathered. That's why you're a friend of Carter's."

I didn't know how to react. She embodied the starkness of Beta City itself.

We walked. Her shoes tapped on the pavement like a fast-paced metronome while the rubber slaps of my sneakers did their best to keep up.

One of those head-to-toe masked beings startled me when he popped out from the side of a building. We halted. Hudson stared into its face.

"The crust is the best part!" he yelled.

Hudson wasn't fazed.

"And a survivor knows the true meaning of the cube," she yelled back.

He let us pass.

"What was that all about?" I asked.

"I have no idea. If they make up shit, so do I." She smirked. "Try it the next time you see one."

"Who are those people?"

"They're playing Enemy Alien."

"In those suits? Virtual reality?"

"Augmented reality," she replied. "The real world is mixed in with the game. Enough for them not to trip over their own feet."

"Why are the suits body-hugging?"

"For the other sensations they feel through the suit. You know, a tingle here, a punch there. It's an all-encompassing alternate reality. The Social Media Central peeps think of everything."

"The game is part of Social Media Central?"

"Tayler, everything is part of Social Media Central. You should know that."

"We never had grey boogeymen shouting weird-arsed comments in Astra City."

"Well, aren't you lucky."

"Is it a new fad?"

"No, Tayler. These freaks have been around for years."

Hudson gestured at the massive red doors of her apartment block. She peered into an eye scanner to the right of the entrance and the doors slid to reveal plush red carpet that met a glass elevator. We entered. Again, she used her pupil for recognition and the elevator opened.

"You seem bitter," I said. She gawped at me as if I'd shat myself. "I mean, you seem like this place has got to you."

She didn't reply. More decadence greeted us inside her residence. Angular modern furniture, high ceilings, and harbour views made this place fancier than my previous lodgings. Hudson strode into this setting as if to the manor born.

Is money no object to her?

She fixed cocktails in the kitchen.

"Blue liquor?" I questioned.

"Don't complain."

I sat on one of the black leather stools at the bench. I thought she'd join me, but Hudson strode to a recliner, kicked off her shoes, and stretched out her legs.

"Now, Tayler. You're curious about me. Why?"

"Because I'm a guest in your home and you're connected to Carter."

She grabbed a tin from inside her leather jacket. I was curious about the image on its lid, so she handed it to me. The picture was of a woman in a long fuzzy pink coat striding past a line of handsome men in navy-blue uniform. Vintage flying machines were in the background, and the word Qantas was stamped in capital letters at the bottom of the image. I handed the tin back.

"It's an old advertisement," Hudson explained, noting my fascination.

Inside was her tobacco and vaper. Smoke with a weird odour soon left a haze around her.

"Yeah, I guess I should tell you something about myself." She dragged slowly as if she was considering what to tell me. "I'm from out of town. The other side of the country, in fact." She stared at me. "You haven't touched your drink."

I sipped.

"Heaven?" she asked. "You look impressed. Like you've made a new friend."

"A delicious friend. What is this?"

"My secret recipe," she replied.

I looked around, admiring her decor. "You're mysterious, Hudson."

"What else would you like to know?"

"Anything."

Her eyes glazed. "I'm the princess in hiding from a country that still calls itself a kingdom. The king and queen top up my bank account monthly even though I left in shame. I was in love with our tailor and our head chef until the day the chef realised I was also making love with the tailor."

"That must be some wicked weed." I loved her imagination.

"It's not marijuana." Hudson let out a steady stream of smoke, which curled into a cloud as it rose. "And who are you, Tayler?"

"Should I share a puff before I answer?"

Her wicked smile faded. "Not for you. This is medicinal, and this blend is expensive." She poked her tongue out. "Who are you, Tayler?"

"I'm a famous artist who fell in love with the model I was painting. My wife didn't approve, so we ran off together but on our first day in Beta City, we stayed with a sculptor. That sculptor won her heart. He is her soulmate. I'm certain."

She shrugged, then inhaled fresh air. She popped her vaper back in the tin and left it on the coffee table. Her eyes widened a little.

"How did you meet Carter?" I asked.

"There's a tale for another time. Come."

She stood and wandered to her balcony. I followed. For the rest of the evening, our conversation stayed in the same vein. I'd ask, she'd answer obscurely, even though she was no longer affected by her weird blend. Hours later, she knew more about me, including my dalliances with Madeline Q and Mike, than I'd expect to tell a stranger. I tried to get her to open up, even encouraging her to smoke so I could chat with the ethereal version of Hudson. But after four weeks of making friends at Cradle Edge, I sat with the Ice Queen, striving to crack her veneer.

She knew little about my fame, or Madi's, through Social Media Central. I deduced she wasn't online much. My time at Cradle Edge taught me I still had anonymity in places, and although Beta City citizens drenched themselves in the all-knowing cyber platform, it stood to reason that a friend of Carter's didn't.

I talked so much to fill the void of her silence, I even self-analysed why I approached sleeping with men and women differently. I hoped she'd have some insight. Why her? Inside her clinical gaze, the cogs were definitely clinking in that analytical mind.

Instead, she took my hand and led me to her bedroom.

She vaped, then stripped her jacket off and threw it on the plush chair in the corner. Next, she leaped on her bed without the covers peeled back. She beckoned me with her long-nailed finger.

Maybe this was the way Hudson shared something of herself. In a city so sterile, perhaps this was the first step to friendship.

We made love, or something close to it.

CHAPTER THREE

HUDSON SPRANG OUT of bed, fumbled around inside the jacket she threw on the chair the previous night, then remembered her vape tin was on her bedside drawers. She'd left it there when we made love. Hudson opened it and lit her first smoke of the day.

"Where are you going?" I asked.

"I'm going to work."

"But aren't you part of the Life Experience Mob? Or at least, you will be when Carter gets here."

"Tayler, dear." She caressed the prickly beard hair under my chin. "How do you think I pay for this swanky apartment? Donations?"

I felt strange. Not because someone who made love with me was leaving. Because for the first time in days I had something resembling human contact, even though her conversation came with a side order of attitude. But I spent too many hours on empty streets being shouted at by random loonies or staring out of windows entertaining my own musings. And now that I would be left alone, I missed Cradle Edge.

"Where do you work?"

She meticulously chose a carrot-toned coat.

"In government. It's not an exciting job but it keeps me in the lifestyle I'm accustomed to."

"Why don't you move away from Beta City? Somewhere that will give you time to enjoy life?"

"I have big plans, Tayler. Now, quiet. I'm late." Regardless of her concern for time, she tried on three different pairs of shoes before deciding on black sneakers. She took a few steps towards her bedroom door, then turned and told me to "Wait here for Carter. He should be here this afternoon." She left her bedroom.

"What time will you be home?"

Her apartment door shut.

As you may have guessed, Hudson dominated the love-making process. And yes, it was a process. A ritual. Each sexual position was held for the right amount of pleasure before she changed to something different. And at each step, it was a body thing. No open-mouthed kissing. Just the jigsaw pieces fitting into the right place with minimal eye contact.

She puffed several times during sex but never offered any. I breathed in as soon as the smoke left her mouth but couldn't get that hazy effect. A little lightheaded, but not the urge to take her shoulders and pin her to the bed as she did with me. It was freaky, kind of "wow", but mostly unsettling.

My love blogger friend, Shaun, would never approve. His motto was "You never really know someone until you make love to them." Going to bed with Hudson wasn't about making love. No. We were fulfilling her need to dominate.

Her fingernail grazed my skin when it made a path from my underarm to my wrist. Her other hand covered my mouth before I could react. She let me moan, running those nails through my hair. I thought I was safe until she clutched me below and demanded I pleasure her. Or more to the point, made me feel like I had a job to do.

Now, alone in her apartment, I pushed my hands into her mattress. Firm. Efficient. I kicked off the sheets that hugged me tight. Crisp. And white enough to have been bleached daily.

I scrambled out of bed. I rubbed my face in anguish, not looking forward to another morning haunted by my own thoughts.

"What am I doing here? Great. Now I'm talking to myself."

I showered, lathering myself in snow-white goat's milk soap. I wrapped myself in fresh clothes before making her bed. I sauntered to the living room and plonked myself on the recliner she sat smoking on the night before. It was then I made sense of something that was physically in front of me. A computer. But it didn't look like a computer.

I'd seen old square television sets created inside make-believe lounge rooms the Life Experience Mob constructed. That was part of a bigger display to teach us of an eccentric historical holiday known as Christmas, with a decorated tree next to the odd cathode ray contraption. Here, at a small desk, was a tubed screen propped up by a long metallic neck.

Like the stem of a plant supporting a flower.

I needed someone willing to chat. I had to contact either Connor or Madeline Q. The keyboard was on the coffee table, so I pulled the screen towards myself. It stayed in place, supported by its malleable stand.

I logged on. Instantly a Social Media Central logo appeared, but not the one I was used to. White design on black screen. Then the home page opened. More white on black, with a line of colour here and there. A dull colour like khaki or maroon.

Okay. I knew I hadn't been near a screen for a while. So, I guess it made sense that Social Media Central had a makeover since the last time I glanced at a screen. But in the pit of my stomach this premise didn't ring true.

In the top right-hand corner was an ad for something called "Reality Wars". The image of a woman's face, saturated in makeup and startled as if she'd caught her husband in bed with a horse, appeared under the bold font. I was tempted to click but I really needed to reconnect with my friends.

I typed "Madi" followed by "Madeline Q" into the search field. Nothing came up. I tried the same words with the phrase "Fashion blog". Again, nothing. Then I tried "Connor" and "Astra City". He was in charge now, yet there was no mention of him on Social Media Central.

I typed "Tayler" and "Astra City". I hit the enter key several times as the words "We can't find anything that matches your query" haunted me.

I slumped, feeling the luxurious cushion on the back of my chair. For about five minutes, or maybe ten, I sat staring at the screen.

This isn't right.

I returned to the home page. I typed "Astra City". Images, but no information or posts from any of its citizens. That's when it dawned on me. I recalled a random game player in his grey clingy suit yelling, "Take me to the centre of the universe!"

This stylised computer with its movable neck felt as if it would come to life, look me in the face with its screen, then proclaim, "I am the centre of the universe. The universe as told in Beta City!"

While living in Astra City, I hardly used Social Media Central. And I definitely didn't look up what was making news in Beta City or any other city for that matter. And here was the irony. With the world, possibly, one click away in any direction on SMC, I never felt more in touch with reality than I had without a screen at Cradle Edge.

"Stop overthinking, Tayler." Just hearing my own voice gave me peace. "But I need to hear myself say this. Social Media Central is fiction as told inside the particular city you have logged in from."

I stood, ready to walk away from this tool of altered realism until the shocked face promoting "Reality Wars" tempted me. I casually slid down the back of the chair, ready to understand something, anything, about this emotionless city.

I clicked. A video began. This was no "shot on portable devices" presentation. This was crisp, clear sound, well-framed images, and orchestrated background music.

That freaky woman and her remarkably skinny husband were entertaining several guests at home. A man in a multicoloured shirt was piling savoury treats from the coffee table onto his plate as he lounged on the settee.

"The black eye?" he said. His voice was unusually soft for a man wearing a bold top. "Nothing to see here. No, really. Although I could say I was defending someone's honour."

The video cut to a two shot of the thin husband and strange wife sharing dubious glances.

Then back to a close-up of the man in a loud shirt. "I was drunk, and I slid down the stairs. Okay?"

Then back to the husband and wife in a room where, now in different clothes, they addressed the camera.

"Our friend, Peter," she began, "likes to chat up unwilling suitors when he's drunk."

"Someone punched him in the eye," the husband added. He leaned closer. "He's just too embarrassed to say."

Back to the party with the camera's gaze on another guest. This was a small lady with crooked teeth, staring into her mobile device as she paced the room.

"Sorry I'm late," she said. "My driver got lost."

Cut to the husband and wife once again addressing the camera directly.

"We've never seen this imaginary driver," he asserted.

"Or her imaginary rich boyfriends who seem to come and go like the seasons."

"Remember when Shelly claimed she couldn't pay her electric bill because someone stole her credit card."

"That credit card was probably lost in a bet." She slowly gave us a sly wink.

Now there was a shot of a third guest with a glass of champagne in hand. Obviously not her first.

"Mother!" she screamed. "It's all about her, you know.

Vicious attacks on my family, including her very own grand-children. Nothing I say or do pleases her. But if she needs to throw a party because my brother has a birthday, or her esteemed woman's club president is paying a visit, then who has to come over and help her with food? And is she ever grateful?"

And so it went. Over the next sixty minutes I learned that the husband was Edward and his wife was Maryanne. They had three sons of which the middle was the favourite, and he knew it. The other two seemed lost as they tried to win their parents' affections. Edward and Maryanne never mentioned their discarded sons in any of their video diaries. And in scenes including them, the parents overlooked the sons' concerns to focus on some minor incident.

Peter was the singer in a band no one came to see, and Edward was never subtle when he used the word "denial" to describe Peter's talents. The champagne guzzler was Frances, and it seemed that even around her mother, a drink was always in her hand. As for Shelly, she flitted in and out of every scene. At one stage, the off-screen director asked if he could follow her home to show the viewers her life. She replied that her place was getting renovated and was overrun in floor samples and fabrics.

Although I was relieved to find some people having a life in Beta City, I was dismayed with Edward and Maryanne's editorial control. Bitchy was the theme for this project.

I'd seen vlogs on Social Media Central. I glanced at historical reality shows from time to time. But here in Beta City, it seemed rich folk professionally documented their own lives for entertainment. Or fame.

As the credits rolled, the thumbnail for the next episode as well as ads for similar videos popped up. I turned off the computer. I craved fresh air.

OUTSIDE, I FOUND a stray human.

"I have to get a snack for my boss," she said. Her eyes, tired and unfocused.

"Where from?" I asked. Food seemed like a good option.

"I'm going home to make her a sandwich."

"Can't she find her own food?"

"That's not the way it works."

She pressed on.

"Stop. I need to talk to someone."

Eventually, she halted, standing still as if she, too, needed emotional contact. She looked my way, eyeing me from head to toe. Then she came closer.

"How long have you worked for your boss?"

I got an odd look. "Since I was a child, of course."

"A child?"

"Where are you from?" she asked.

"Astra City."

"Don't your parents sell you to your boss where you come from?" she asked. "So you'll have a good job when you grow up?"

"Alien space probes are a menace to society," came a voice from the distance.

We both looked. She shrugged and walked away. I headed towards the vague sentence, knowing what I'd find yet oddly wanting to be near more humans.

Two grey-suited beings were looking up a tree where a beagle had been placed on a wooden platform and tied to a branch. He even had a kennel on the scaffold and seemed unfazed by his circumstance.

"Where do you think this one came from, Captain?" One of the beings pointed to the dog. "The Wattle-tree people or the computations of the realm."

Computations of the realm? Does that even make sense?

"Equations stump me, old friend. Calculus. Algorithms. Pi. But the computations bring us closer to our cause."

Someone had to save the dog from this silliness. As I climbed onto a branch, it snarled at me.

"It has teeth, Captain. This space probe has teeth!"

I wandered away.

I SLEPT. NOT because I was tired. So I could kill a few hours. It was just after twelve. I was hoping Carter would arrive soon.

I logged on again, clicking on the Enemy Alien logo that was now in the top right-hand corner. A live stream played, switching between several cameras. All were focused on a cylindrical probe sitting on a metallic platform up a tree. I heard it make a muffled bark. Then its bark turned into beeps and whistles as it moved back and forth on its base. As one of the cameras followed it, I realised the moving image was beamed from one of the players. All these streamed images came directly from their suits.

Who is vision switching? Perhaps Social Media

Central has software to do it itself?

I closed the game and was suddenly greeted with a picture of me. The ad in the corner now promoted the Radical Faith Alliance and there I was framed within a chocolate-brown graphic. I clicked.

YOU HAVE A RIGHT TO AMBITION. YOU
HAVE A RIGHT TO STATUS. YOU HAVE A
RIGHT TO DREAM!

What the fuck?

I was in the foreground of this graphically designed message. My name spelt out in stylised angular letters with the phrase "Dream with me" floating towards the screen in an old-fashioned three-dimensional effect.

The front door opened.

"You're back early," I said to Hudson. "There's no sign of Carter, but it's only lunchtime."

"I didn't expect you to use the computer."

"What else is there to do?"

She peered at the screen. "Would you like wine?" she asked, still examining what I was logged on to.

"Wine. Yes, please." I stood up, pointing at my image. "What do you know about the Radical Faith Alliance?"

"Master," she yelled. "Trouble!"

A wall of Perspex shot up, separating us. I smelled gas. A mask dropped from the kitchen ceiling. She placed it over her mouth. White mist rose from my feet, and while I was impressed that all this happened with her basic voice command, my eyes stung before my world went black.

CHAPTER FOUR

A CLOTH WITH a pungent odour was placed under my nostrils to wake me.

"What the hell are you doing here?" I screamed.

He was the first thing I saw when I woke. My arch nemesis. Stuart Manning, in the flesh.

He grinned like he was showing off a new set of dentures. His pleasure in apprehending me was sickening.

Back in Astra City, he had been in power. The elected official, supposedly. He used Social Media Central to make out he was doing his job. But all he was doing was playing its citizens like a puppeteer, having fun at society's expense.

I was tied to a chair, shaking, and momentarily distracted by a view. Outside the window of this penthouse apartment was the section of the harbour with jets of water dancing in syncopated patterns. Each individual spurt had its own light, which changed to multiple hues of the same colour. They even created an authentic shade of gold, which alternated with sunflower-yellow and mustard. And even though Hudson and my rental accommodation had a harbour view, this vantage point was much more opulent.

Where am I? What part of town is this?

The stone bridges weaved around lofty glass skyscrapers. Each sported a white road with black lines, contrary to any other highway I'd seen. And to the side, an old track accompanied the network of bridgework, but I couldn't work out what it was for.

"I can tell you're impressed." Stuart sat at his dining table, cutting into a steak, making my mouth water. "Welcome to my home, Tayler."

"Why are you here, in Beta City?"

He gestured to the admirable view. "This is my kingdom."

"Your kingdom?"

"I'm the Government here," he announced through a cheesy grin.

"You're what?" My sudden movement made my chair jump. "After you screwed up in Astra City, you're in charge of Beta City?"

"Someone believed in me."

"Or was stupid enough to give you a second chance. Tell me, how are you controlling the citizens this time? I've seen this version of Social Media Central. You've created something called the Radical Faith Alliance. And my picture is on the graphic. What's your plan? Do you even have a plan?"

"You're tied to a chair, Tayler. Should you address me

like that?"

"I've gotten away with it in the past. And you're using *my* image for a reason, so I know you want me alive."

"True." He chomped on his steak, ignoring the salad at the side of his plate. "And it's killing you not knowing why you're the face of my secret plan."

"A plan that preaches hope, ambition, and the right to dream? Damn right it's killing me. Just what are you up to?"

He stood. His lips were splattered with gravy while he clutched what was left of his steak. "Hungry?"

He strolled to me and shoved the gnawed bone in my face. I turned my head, but he pushed it against my mouth. Tiny bits of medium-rare flesh tempted me. The seasoned taste was on my lips, and before I knew it, I caved in, biting the sparse bits of Stuart's leftovers like a prisoner of war.

He went back to his table and returned with the napkin he used. He wiped my mouth, smearing the juices over my face.

"I knew you were hungry," he sneered. He threw the bone and the napkin on his plate and strolled to the window with the view. He peered out at his territory.

"Where's Carter?" I asked.

"I don't know. Have you misplaced him?"

"You *knew* he was going to meet me," I surmised.

He gazed blankly at me. *What is he thinking?*

He said, "Where are my manners? I should show you around my city. You haven't experienced this part of town."

"You're avoiding my question."

"You don't expect me to answer, Tayler."

"You could at least put me in the picture. Let me know what you have planned with me and the Radical Faith

Alliance. Tell me where Carter is. Tell me how Hudson is part of this."

"You're nosey, my friend."

I huffed. "I have a right to know."

"So you think."

I gritted my teeth.

"Let me prepare transport for your trip around the city." He opened his front door. "See you soon." He exited the penthouse.

I pushed my feet as hard as I could against the floor, making the chair hop. My biceps chafed painfully against the wooden cross-rails, but I had to loosen the restraint around my wrists. I felt rope burn. I changed tack, and somehow, in my frenzied frustration, the rope slackened.

"Come on," I said to myself. "You can do it."

The back of my hands rubbed against one another like two sticks determined to make fire. A little more wiggle room. I pulled them apart again. The knot stayed in place.

The front door opened. Stuart drifted in like a ghost ready to torment me.

"Your chariot awaits," he said.

Once again, I drifted into slumber. This time from the chemically soaked handkerchief he forced over my face.

"YOU'RE AWAKE, TAYLER."

Through my blurry, blinking eyes, I saw Stuart standing next to a large lever. We were in a concrete room. I was tied to something cold and metallic. It was the front seat of a roller coaster.

"This hasn't been used in a while," he said. "Recreation is an outdated concept. I have too many worker bees in this city who don't have time for carnival rides. And those with time prefer, well, you've seen them in their stretchy head-to-toe suits."

The lever made a crunch when Stuart yanked it towards him. Two doors swung open as my roller coaster jolted as if lurching off its rails. More unearthly clanking and my ride was off.

One of my arms was over the safety rail, the other was under it, with my wrists still tied together. I kept my fingers entwined so I could pull the rail towards myself to keep some sort of grip.

I now knew what the track beside the bridge was for. I whisked around skyscrapers as the screech of my rusted vehicle kept my fear factor high.

"Has Sabastian eaten his cornflakes?" The shouting voice came from behind me, but with my hands twisted around the guard rail, I couldn't look without breaking my fingers. "I said 'Has Sabastian had breakfast?'"

My ride swerved, causing pain in my knuckles. My arse slammed against the seat. The gamer shot at the empty road to our side, causing puffs of concrete dust to explode off the pristine white street.

A woman stared up at me as I plummeted towards her. Then the carriage swerved again. Her scream echoed as we zoomed through a cavity of a steel tower. Clerks stared from the windows. Shots rang out, shattering glass. *What is this nitwit doing?*

A sudden rise and a monumental fall. My fingers ached, pressing against the rod harder. Skin and bone against metal. *My joints will break!*

Water! We sped into the harbour. The tracks left the accompanying road and hung over the sea. We swerved once more. Wind dried my face. Air cracked my lips. I was a ball in a pinball machine winding through the obstacles, praying I wouldn't smash into anything.

"Ugh." I was nauseous.

Another skyscraper. Another random person staring at two lunatics on a rocky rail. Another team of suits gazing from their office.

"I don't think Sabastian's eaten breakfast."

"I don't care if Sabastian's eaten breakfast," I yelled. "Who the hell cares if he's had corn flakes or porridge or eggs on toast."

The city blurred. The building to my right seemed familiar. The dancing fountains whirled and whirled and... I thought I might be sick.

Breathe! Close your eyes. Breathe!

A shudder. My carriage rocked. The doors swung open. Stuart. It was Stuart. Nasty evil Stuart. The concrete room. A sudden jolt. We stopped.

"Argh!" My crunching fingers. The spinning room. The spinning concrete room. The whirling, spinning, out of control, nauseating churn of my stomach.

I lost consciousness until discordant carnival music woke me to the looniest confrontation I ever faced.

CHAPTER FIVE

"STEP RIGHT UP, folks. Spin the wheel. Win your free-dom."

This irritating voice spoke over the annoying sideshow music.

There was a prize wheel and other weird shit in a place that looked nothing like Stuart's penthouse.

The vast ceiling, walls, and floor were painted red, and just for a bit of added colour, a gelato cart was situated two metres from where I was tied and elevated, crucifix style. Plus, I was stripped down to my underwear. My clothes were nowhere in sight.

A gamer in an augmented reality suit tended the cart while a couple of others mimed licking pretend ice cream cones while watching me.

Another gamer laid his hand on the wheel and spoke with the charisma of a game show host. "Sabastian is our only contestant, and we know he's dying to take a chance on his fate. Or maybe dying is his fate?"

He spun the prop. The wheel whirled with a sound like fast-tapping fingernails, yet there were no words written on it. Only colours which matched the flavours of the gelato options on the cart.

"Pistachio, folks! Sabastian's fate is in synch with a nut. A delicious green nut with a frustrating shell."

"I'm not Sabastian," I shouted. "I'm Tayler. Cold, sick of this place Tayler!"

"Please be quiet. We have to see what pistachio means for someone like you." He wheeled out a cathode ray tube monitor from behind the wheel. The screen shone green. He bent over, placed a pair of imaginary glasses over his nose, and read words that didn't exist from the display. "Pistachio alone is not to be trusted unless it's teamed with vanilla. But beware of chocolate." He spun the wheel again.

Cold balls smashed over my body. I smelled the pistachio but couldn't reach any of it with my mouth. The gelato-tending gamer returned to his cart with his used ice cream scoop.

"Ah, vanilla. You're a lucky man, Sabastian. You get to eat this one."

The show host gamer struggled with a large metal ladder. Then, the ice cream vendor climbed the ladder and shoved his scoop under my face. Whatever the white stuff was, it didn't smell of vanilla. He pressed it to my lips.

My stomach growled. I opened my mouth. Refrigerated mashed potato! I ate with equal parts wanting and disgust, hungry enough to swallow the unseasoned mess.

"Stuart, where are you?" My tongue was as dry as sandpaper. "What is the point of all this? Payback for defeating you in Astra City?"

"Now, now, Sabastian. You overstepped the mark." The gamer slid the ladder away, making an irritating judder against the floor. He flicked my big toe with his fingernail. "You wouldn't share your lair with your comrades." He flicked a middle toe. "And you know we're a band of brothers and sisters with a cause." He flicked my smallest toe. "The Enemy Alien must be defeated, and your lair is our meeting place." He squeezed my foot, hard. "And I still hate you for sleeping with my girlfriend."

He flittered back to the wheel. *He has a girlfriend? With a walk like that he has a girlfriend?*

He spun. The colours blurred as the TV screen flashed hues at seizure-inducing intervals.

"Ah, chocolate." He shook his head. So did the others in the room, until one spoke up.

"But chocolate after vanilla after pistachio doesn't mean an execution."

"Are you sure?" The host stared at the screen as if it displayed instructions. "Can we at least neuter him, so he doesn't stray again?"

"You're getting extremely riled up over an imaginary character," I reasoned.

"Imaginary? You're here, Sabastian, aren't you? Up on a pedestal—"

"A pedestal! I'm on a fucking crucifix. And I'm not Sabastian. I'm Tayler." I wrestled with my restraints. "Get me off here."

"Now, where were we? That's right. Chocolate." He faced the gelato vendor. "Do you have anything besides a scoop or ice cream in your cart? Anything sharp, maybe?"

"I have a blender for mixing fruit with cream, but the blades are attached to the base of the machine."

"Could we frappé Sabastian's balls in it?"

The gamer gazed at my underwear. "His toolset isn't big enough to reach the blades if we dangle them inside the blender."

"Could we try? Is there an extension cord?"

"What the hell!" I tried to yank myself loose. "I'm not Sabastian, you jerks! I'm Tayler. I'm here from Cradle Edge. Sabastian is a figment of your imagination."

"Feisty, isn't he?" The vendor searched inside a compartment of his cart. He pulled out his ice cream scoop. "We could slap his balls with this."

"No," said the show host. "I have a better idea. Scoop some gelato."

He did. A ball of bacio was ready for the host's twisted plan. The scoop was handed to him, and he thrust the ladder back in place. He climbed it, tugged my underwear open, and examined me.

"That's what you used on my girlfriend? How did you satisfy her with that?"

"Yikes!" Icy dairy dessert dissolved against my balls and my cotton briefs. The milky goo dripped down my legs and onto the crimson floor.

"It looks like you've soiled yourself." The show host shook his arms in the air in victory while still on the ladder. He pushed against the crotch of my undies, freezing my privates even more.

"You just wanted to cop a feel," I said. "You don't really have a girlfriend."

He grinned. "I did and I do." He licked his fingers and jumped off the ladder, kicking it aside. "Time to spin the wheel."

It landed on Amaretto Cherry.

"Do you have that flavour?" the host asked.

"I have every flavour." The vendor grabbed the handles of his cart and wheeled it towards me. His pretend customers followed.

"Stuart!" I yelled. "I give in. Take me down from here because this is insane."

The vendor handed ice cream scoops to the others, so they picked a flavour, scooped it, and flung it at me.

I was an abstract painting. Confectionery colours dribbled across my human canvas. Spheres of frost hit hard, chilled me, then oozed down my skin like squirts of excessive sunscreen.

"Enough already, Stuart! Call off your kooks. I'll leave Beta City right away. Just let me clean up first. Ouch. That one had fudge pieces. Let me go and I'll leave in peace. Ouch. Frozen cherries sting! Stop it. Stuart. Stuart."

The gamers fell to the ground as if their power had been shut off. *But there are people inside those suits. How?*

Stuart entered from behind me.

"Were you here the whole time?" I asked.

"I was near, but not in this room." He fingered a glob of limone from my knee and sampled it like a chef determining what spice to add to the pot. "Sour. I never thought you'd taste sour."

"What was the point of all this?"

"Why? Don't you like ice cream?"

"Stuart, this was crazy shit. What on earth were you trying to prove?"

"That this place is crazier than Astra City, Tayler, and if you change your mind and don't leave, then Beta City is going to get weirder for you."

I shook my head. "No, Stuart. That's not what this display was for. You wanted to show me you're in charge. You wanted to play with me. Put on a show for me. Put me in my place..." I studied my technicolour body. "You wanted to show me the type of madness these gamers love." I gazed at the sleeping kooks. "Have they got something to do with the Radical Faith Alliance?"

Stuart flipped the collar of his knee-length coat upwards around his neck, creating a focal point to his face.

"Tayler." He patted my thigh. "Tayler. Tayler. Tayler. I'm not finished with you yet. I know you miss Cradle Edge. Your boyfriend and your girlfriend are probably missing you back home in Astra City. But when Stuart has plans, Tayler must wait."

He swirled on the heel of his shoe and faced the opposite direction. He inspected the unconscious deadbeats, feeling each for a pulse. One murmured. Stuart nodded. He strolled to the gelato cart and fished out a gas mask and a pink ball from the compartment. He stared into my eyes as he placed the mask over his own head. Then he aimed a small pink ball below my ice-cream-splattered altar.

Mist shot out as soon as it hit the floor. I choked. This wasn't good. My eyes stung. I foolishly inhaled, expecting fresh air to fill my lungs, but this vapour smelt like paint thinner. And it burned my throat. I held my breath, but the room was already spinning. A tear, then another, weaved down my cheeks. I was on a merry-go-round of mad adventures with my nemesis and a cast of Sabastian-loving losers.

I closed my eyes and gave in.

CHAPTER SIX

I WOKE, TIED to the same chair from Stuart's apartment, yet I was outside. And I was dressed, fresh, with no remnants of sticky gelato on my skin. *Who washed me?*

The tree with the beagle was right in front of me. Three game players watched the dog as it kept a keen eye on them. It strolled back and forth, patrolling its own living quarters from the mad augmented reality team.

"Why are we here?" I asked.

"The alien space probe is thinking," said one of the fools.

"It has to be destroyed." Stuart eyed me while caressing the lapels of his knee-length coat.

A shot was fired. The beagle yelped. Another shot was fired. The dog shrieked before collapsing. I couldn't believe my eyes. A living thing had been murdered. *But why?* My shock alternated with bursts of anger.

"Toughen up," said one of the game players.

I cried. The three in grey left, all in different directions.

"See, Tayler." Stuart sneered. "I still have control over *you*, and *my* augmented army."

I gasped between the tears with no way of wiping my face. Stuart didn't speak. Eventually, I did.

"I don't know where to begin. Do I scream at you for the act of terror you were part of, or do I ask you why, knowing you'll say something pathological?"

"No need to ask anything." I swear he danced on the spot. "You see, Tayler, the game gives the public the illusion of control in their workaholic lives. I've created the Beta City I need, while they invent the Beta City they want, separately. Two realities happening at once."

"But why be so cruel?" As soon as I said this, I remembered that back in Astra City, he was behind the murder of someone I came to know. The question was redundant.

"Governments either unite a society or turn it in on itself. This city needs to be subservient. It serves my goals. A lot of people fear walking the streets because of the Enemy Alien game. It freaks them out."

This was classic Stuart. For him, it was domination at all costs. Or so I thought, until he crouched to untie my hands from the back of my seat.

"Why are you...?" I murmured. My hands were free.

"I have the power, and this time, you don't have anyone here to help you overthrow me."

"What have you done with Carter? You have him, don't you?"

Three more grey-clad game players were marching back. One lifted his gun.

"Run, Tayler," Stuart yelled. "Run!"

I did. The chair flew back as I charged at the speed of fear. I stumbled a little, but my legs weren't going to let my groggy state hinder my escape. Shots were fired, but I didn't look back. Designer buildings whisked past. Sunlight reflected in windows. *Morning? It's morning!* There were three distinct rhythms to their chase. I changed course, sprinting down a street.

I zigzagged through as many random paths as I could. The architecture was different. Shabby. The city was now shabby. I ran into the open door of a three-storey dwelling. An empty elevator was waiting. In I went, hitting the top floor button over and over again. Finally, it moved. My back pressed against the cracked mirror surface inside, and I sunk until my butt found the floor. I puffed like a steam train.

When the doors opened, I jumped out and lay on the musty carpet. The place smelt like cheese melts and masturbation, but it was heaven after all the drama I had just dealt with. My sweat sank into its weave.

"Who are you?"

The voice was male. Rich and low. I raised my head. The voice belonged to a brown-skinned dude. Yes, dude was the best way to describe him. He was as young as me with short back and sides. His left nostril sported a nose ring. He was cool to my geek. I reached to offer my hand.

"I'm Tayler."

He shook it.

"I'm Sage."

"Sage? You're the first person I've ever met named Sage."

He helped lift me off the ground.

"What are you doing here?" he asked.

"I'm running from maniacs."

"So, you're not here to see anyone?"

"No."

"You're trespassing?"

"No, Sage. I'm staying safe."

He stepped back.

"You're not here to see someone, so—"

"Listen! I'm on the run. Do you know Stuart Manning?"

"Yeah, man, everyone knows him. He's the Government."

"He's after me."

Sage grinned approvingly. "What did you do?"

"Before I answer, I need to ask. You don't recognise me, do you? You've never heard of me on Social Media Central?"

He shook his head.

"Boy, have I got a story for you." I continued blabbering, eventually talking my way into safety inside his flat.

"Glass of water?" he asked.

"Glass of water," I replied.

Laundry was strung on rope attached to picture hooks. Mould was prevalent, especially on some spots of the rotting floorboards. And this singular room creaked even when no one moved.

"That's the people downstairs," Sage explained. "They walk. My place creaks."

"Spooky," I replied.

He gestured to his tan vinyl lounge. I sat. A long crack

in the covering scratched against my back. He opened his fridge. Its door creaked too. His mattress had sunk, and its exposed worn springs added to the eeriness of his apartment. He grabbed something from his refrigerator.

"You had a cold glass already filled with water in your fridge?"

He opened its door wider. Most shelves held numerous glasses of water. There must have been forty or so all up.

"I can't afford to stock my fridge," he replied. "So, tap water it is. I refill when I drink and put them back to chill. And when I'm hungry, I drink glass after glass."

"You can't only live on water."

"My neighbours bring leftovers from time to time."

"You don't have a job," I concluded.

"I work at night."

"What do you do?"

"Call centre for the stupid."

"Oh, I see. Sage, you've lost faith in humanity."

"Man, I reckon you have too."

I told my story. I talked about my famous friends on Social Media Central—well, at least Astra City's version of Social Media Central—and how I'd become well known through association. He was surprised to hear Stuart Manning was once the Government of my city, and I told him I was just as shocked to find Stuart in Beta City. But trying to explain how he used social media to frame my friends for a murder made Sage cross his arms and stare at me as if I'd just claimed the world was flat.

"Come on, Tayler! Really?"

"You have no idea how evil the man is."

"Hey, I like my conspiracy theories. Most of that stuff

on Social Media Central is bull. What I read today doesn't match what I read two years ago. But Stuart isn't on anyone's radar. He doesn't have a profile on SMC. He's a quiet insignificant."

"A quiet insignificant?"

"Yeah. He appeared over a year ago to keep the wheels turning. He's insignificant. Quietly insignificant."

I studied Sage's face. He wore a calm bitterness, if that even made sense. He was a battler and didn't concern himself with things until he had to. I think. There was no way for me to know. These were my first impressions of him. I was sure he'd never be a friend. *So why did I tell him my story?*

"Tayler, you're an odd duck."

"An odd duck. Out of all the phrases to come out of your mouth, that wasn't one I expected."

"You finished your water. Do you want another?"

"If you think I'm an odd duck, why haven't you asked me to leave?"

"I will." He fetched another glass.

"What's your story?" I asked.

"No story. I work like a slave to stay in this apartment. Just like everyone else in the slums."

"What do you do for kicks?"

"Hook up." He laughed as he read my face. "What else is there in an anonymous city?"

"Men, women, or both?"

"Men." He smirked. "My weakness."

"Your addiction."

"My way to survive."

"What about intimacy?"

Sage went quiet.

"Sorry," I said. "I didn't mean to pry."

"Why is Stuart after you?"

"Hold on. You think Stuart's a *quiet insignificant*, even though you seemed delighted I was hiding from him before."

"I invited you in to hear a conspiracy theory. That's all."

"Sage, how do you log on to Social Media Central?" He pulled his device from his jean pocket. "Look up the Radical Faith Alliance."

"Yeah, the counter religion that preaches hope. Please! Save us from stupidity."

"Counter religion? Sage, counter religion to what?"

He stared at me as if I had two heads.

"Entrepreneurship," he replied.

"Since when is entrepreneurship a religion?"

"Duh. Since, like, all my life." He huffed, as though he was expelling his burdens in that breath. "My folks paid into it so I could work. Have a job. Pay for things."

"Like food?"

He seemed annoyed. "Man, what rock do you live under? If people don't pay into Entrepreneurship, then their kids won't have a job."

"So that's the only way to have a job?"

"Man, it's the only way to have a boss. Entrepreneurship makes sure I have the same boss for life. I worked for him since I was sixteen."

I had goosebumps. "And it's called a religion?"

He didn't answer. He trembled, as if the adult I was speaking to was now a child. As if that child was haunted by experiences he was too innocent to understand. Or as if my line of questioning sowed irreversible doubt. But again, I wasn't sure.

He curled himself into a ball. I went to him, crouching and gently rubbing my hand on his back. His hand reached for his hair, and his finger wrapped itself inside one of his curls. He was deep inside himself, lost with no way to come out.

His deathly stare unnerved me. I caressed his shoulders, coaxing him back with intimacy. He dropped his head and gazed down between his legs.

"Where were you, Sage?"

"Life is overwhelming, man. I'm sorry you saw that."

"Are you usually alone when this happens?"

He nodded. "The Radical Faith Alliance is a new thing," he explained, as if his dissociation never happened. "It showed up on Social Media Central two days ago. A few of us are suspicious. Revolution? Talk of hope? No, something's up."

"Where did you find people to speak to? I've been here for days and no one's around."

"We spoke online."

"Oh. Then why don't you recognise my face from the Radical Faith Alliance logo?"

"There's no face on the logo."

"Yes, there is!"

His device was on the floor, not far from us. I reached for it, and he fired it up.

"Tayler, your face wasn't here before. Are you some missing messiah of the faith?" He smirked at his own humour. "No, seriously, why are you the face of this?"

"I don't know. But at least I now know why Stuart let me go. He has a plan. What am I saying? Stuart never has a thought-out plan. Just ideas. He'll make it up as he goes along. Until then, I'm hiding."

"From Stuart?"

"From those fucking nitwits in grey suits who think I'm the Enemy Alien!"

Sage looked angered. "I didn't invite you to stay."

"But I just comforted you."

He shook his head.

"Sage, please. Just for tonight. Tomorrow, I'll devise a plan for saving my friend, Carter."

"Tayler, you have more twists and turns than an acid trip." He noted my smile. "No, Tayler. My humour is no sign for you to stay. I don't know you."

"You don't know the random strangers you let in for sex."

"There's something in it for me. What have you got to offer? And don't say sex."

I grinned, although I didn't mean to.

"What about conversation?" I argued. "You don't chat to your sex partners the way you do with me. Do you?"

"No, but man, you're getting too close."

I opened my mouth, but no words followed. I had no idea what to say. I stood.

"Thanks," I murmured.

I strolled to the exit and stopped at the door. I searched for meaning to his lack of empathy. I slammed the door of his flat. I pressed the button on the elevator but when it arrived, I decided not to take it. I sat on the pungent carpet, ready to spend the night in the hall.

"Our army is strong. The Enemy Alien will not eat, sleep, or relieve himself in the eyes of our leader."

"Oh, for goodness' sake!" I yelled.

Instantly I knew my exclamation was a dumb idea. There, entering from the fire escape, were two of those spandex-clad weirdos.

CHAPTER SEVEN

I RAN PAST them. What else could I do? I swiftly shot down the stairs. More grey figures were waiting outside the building.

"Are you the Master Blaster?" one asked me.

"No, jackass," replied another. "He's the Enemy Alien!"

As I lurched for speed, I was tripped. The gravel clawed my stomach. I was too tired to whimper.

Three more ventured out of Sage's building. They must have been combing each floor.

"So, he's not the Master Blaster?"

"Who is the Master Blaster?" asked one who'd just come outside.

"The doppelganger of the alien enemy," said another. I knew the voice. *Could I be right?* "He's the good one sent here to take the place of his double, once we've captured the alien."

"Good. Bad. Everything in between will be learned from both the Master Blaster and the Enemy Alien."

"I could be the Master Blaster," I said. I tried not to chuckle over the absurdity.

"Yes, keep them both alive."

The one with the familiar voice helped me up. We all walked for about twenty minutes, past more of the slums. Timber houses with peeling paintwork were wedged between solid brick buildings with no character. Cracked cement apartments with no front door urged the residents to leave the entrance light on so trespassers could be seen in the shadows. And here and there a dog barked as another pointless sentence was spoken.

We finally stopped at a red stone building that looked like a store. Its door and window frames were chaotically constructed from untreated timber. The stairs creaked like Sage's studio apartment as we made our way to the first floor.

"Are you sure he's not the Master Blaster?"

"I thought the Master Blaster was someone different."

They forced me to sit on a lone chair as they continued their mindless banter, which, by this stage, I'd stopped listening to. They were, however, surrounding me in a perfect circle, and none of them seemed to have a gun. There were two ways out of this room. The way we came in and through a door that was currently closed. *Perhaps there's a whole apartment through that door. With a set of fire stairs out the back.*

"I am the Master Blaster," I said, randomly.

"But there's a shadow in your midst," one of the grey clones replied.

"Seriously, I am the good one," I said. "The Master Blaster."

"The hyena was on my mind that day. He was a good animal. He displayed courage."

I stood. That's when I realised my initial observation was wrong. One had a gun.

I placed my palm over my chest and stated with authority, "I am the Master Blaster!"

"But his laugh is what gives him away," said the gunman. "And at just the right pitch it will shatter glass."

"Does the hyena have a sense of humour?" I asked.

"No. He's way too concerned with the problems of the world. He laughs to release himself from his own anguish."

I lowered myself steadily onto the chair, my head reeling from the nonsense. The gun was put away, so I tuned out of the insane dialogue until its monotonous tone put me to sleep.

"TAYLER, WAKE UP," said the one with the familiar voice.

"It is you!"

He took off his headpiece and still gave me attitude as opposed to a smile.

"You wouldn't let me stay and now you're my saviour. What made you come after me, Sage?"

"Once I heard them in the hall, well, man, I figured what you said could be true."

The others were asleep on the floor.

"What time is it?" I asked.

"Not sure. It's dark."

A few were snoring.

"They sleep in their suits?" I asked.

"Tayler, they live in them. It keeps the pain of society away."

"Don't they work?"

"When they have to."

"And they spend all their money on their suits and this silly game?" I queried.

He held his headpiece in front of my face. "These are free."

One of the players was sleeping in front of the stairs. I headed towards him. Sage stopped me.

"What are you doing?" he asked.

"Getting out of here."

"Tayler, there'll be more outside."

Sage pointed to the door at the side of the room. We cautiously sneaked through. It was a storeroom with only a few boxes on several shelves.

"Whose shop is this?" I whispered.

He shrugged. "They took you here. I followed." He listened for noise, briefly, then looked me in the eye and said, "Now strip!"

"Huh?"

From under his arm he unzipped his springy augmented reality suit.

"Tayler, you have to disappear. Swap clothes so you'll be one of *them*."

"Cougar pie is only nice when covered in flat lemonade," I said.

"What?" Sage asked.

"I'm practising my pointless dialogue."

We switched attire. Sage helped me zip up his outfit.

"Oh my," I muttered.

"Camels have the run of the pack," he said.

I lifted my facial cover above my ears. "Did you just say, 'Camels have the run of the pack'?" He gave me a cheeky look. I put the mask back on.

The storeroom had alien probes watching me from each shelf. Sage's mouth gave off light as he yawned. I tilted my head and saw I was clad in golden armour.

"Am I a soldier or a robot?" I asked. "Actually, don't answer."

CHAPTER EIGHT

"IS THERE A beetle that speaks with an accent?"

I wasn't sure who said this until it was repeated. It was evident from the light coming from his mouth that it was the one blocking the staircase. He was lying on his side, elbow on the floor while propping his head in the palm of his hand.

"What accent in particular?" I asked.

"A little Turkish. A little like the phrasing of a moth."

I seriously didn't know what to say next.

He sat up. Sage sat next to him.

"You're not familiar with the dialect of a moth?" he asked.

"It's like the rantings of a mule when the moon is new," Sage said.

"I have to pass you both and go downstairs," I reasoned.

"One of those probes travelled down there."

He stood. Behind his back, Sage was gesturing frantically to the storeroom.

"Actually, there's a horde of them behind that door," I said and pointed just as frantically.

He marched towards the imaginary enemy and entered as Sage grabbed me and ran downstairs. We heard gunshots followed by the others stumbling about. Outside, I took off my mask.

"Don't be an idiot, man!" Sage griped. "That's what's keeping you alive. Stay inside the game."

He pulled it back over my head.

As we roamed, we didn't speak. I was amazed at how different my world was. The slums had changed into a city of gems. Each window didn't appear like glass, but like an exotic stone glimmering in the moonlight. I looked up. The moon was not the moon. It was a silver ball. *A sphere housing a community in the sky, perhaps? Or is this where the Enemy Alien hails from?*

Then I saw small shapes circling the globe and knew more probes were on their way. A vehicle shot by. I focused on it and saw a hovering craft with two slithery beings riding it. I tried taking off my mask to seek clarity, but Sage pressed against my neck to stop it being peeled off.

"What do I look like to them?" I asked.

Sage didn't answer as I shivered, orgasmically. A thousand tiny fingers massaged me from each point of my body. I groaned. My vision was blurring, but I made out the light from my companion's mouth and knew he was laughing. I didn't care. I was in ecstasy.

"What's happening?" I asked.

My penis was stirring. As a huge wave of intense pleasure shot from my head to my toe, my dick stood to full glory.

And just as quickly, the sensation stopped.

I felt faint. Sage held me as I kept my balance. He sat me down on a huge mechanical tortoise as I tried again to take off my mask. He wagged his finger in front of my face. I left my mask on.

My own sense of self returned, and we made our way past more jewelled structures, back to a stone cave with a mouth for an entrance.

"Where are we?" I asked.

Another stone mouth waited for us inside, and as we entered, Sage took off my mask.

We were in his elevator. I sighed in relief. Soon, I was back on his crusty couch and in my own clothes.

"What was that orgasmic rush all about?"

He grabbed a cold glass of water from his fridge and handed it to me.

"It's how the players stay hooked." He sat on his mattress, a safe distance from me.

"So, there's more to this senseless game than silly phrases and shooting live things. There's sexual satisfaction for nerds who aren't getting any."

Sage had the perfect grin for my revaluation. A wicked smile, which framed his milk-coloured teeth.

"And I bet you love being around those nerds when they get aroused," I added.

"Were you thinking of me in your sex rush, Tayler?"

"You wish, dude boy." I sipped. "So, what do I look like inside the game?"

"Like a mean mess shooting lasers from your eyes."

"So, if I have lasers, why aren't they scared of me?"

"Trust me, man. You look like a pussy."

I strolled to a window so I could see his neighbourhood without the fantasy coating. Even in the dark, it was shoddy as hell. A cracked light opposite was the only globe on the street. It shot a harsh beam into the windows of a rundown dwelling, making me wonder if the people inside could sleep even with the curtains drawn. The moon was the moon again. It wasn't even a full moon, which made me wonder how the augmented reality game determined its reinvention of the world.

"You're stuck here, aren't you, Sage?"

"You know my story."

"You're your boss's property."

"You got it."

"Why don't you leave?" I could feel his eyes on me. "I could take you to Cradle Edge."

I faced him. He had a look of true horror. As if the Grim Reaper just tapped him on the shoulder.

"Families get arrested if we leave. Or they disappear."

"Are you sure?"

"You see it all the time."

"On Social Media Central?" I asked.

"Sometimes. But I know people whose..."

I extended my arms for a hug, but he backed away. I sat with him on his mattress instead.

"I didn't mean to pry, Sage."

He shot up. "You have no idea what it's like here. And you can't leave because they've got you. This city keeps you. You're at its whim." He shook his head. "Sorry, man. I'm out of line. I'm out of line."

He paced, like an automated vacuum making sure it cleaned every inch of floor. And he was no longer here with me but in some shadowy place inside his head.

I, too, felt alone. He was my only contact in Beta City, and he was lost in himself. I lay back. I thought I'd derive some sense of security from this action. Something soft giving me comfort, or more to the point, me forcing comfort onto myself.

He halted, standing half a metre away.

"They spit on us," he said. "When we're in their part of the city, they know who we are and they spit on us."

"But you're all part of the same city."

"No, Tayler. It's us and them. And they own us. Really own us. And when my family paid for me to have a boss, they owned them as well."

"And they call this a religion?"

"A religion that keeps us in place."

"Like all religions. Or so I've read. I never encountered a religion in Astra City." I sat up. "Who is your god?"

"God? What's a god? What are you talking about? Man, you *live* in altered reality!"

This was way too sinister. Did Sage even know what the word "religion" meant? I patted the spot next to me on the mattress, but he looked away.

"Hey, Sage. Why have you got an augmented reality suit?"

"To stay sane." He sat on the floor and wrapped his arms around his knees. "I don't think about the call centre when I play. Or food. And if I'm with the nerds, they won't break into my home."

"They break into homes?" I frowned. "What a stupid

question. Of course, they do. They came to get me."

"They only go to the entrance. Coming for a person is not normal."

"I saw them shoot a dog."

"I saw that too. It's never happened before."

"But they shoot at things."

"Never to kill. The software in these suits won't allow it."

"But they shot at me, Sage."

"And they missed at close range. Until that dog. Something's changed."

"This game is Stuart Manning's law enforcement."

Sage finally joined me on the mattress.

"Tell me something else," I said. "Why does your building look like a cave with an open mouth, inside the game?"

His eyes widened. "It doesn't."

My fear rose. Stuart had made Sage's building stand out. He knew this was where I was hiding. *Was my voice recognised from inside the game?*

Sage's apartment door came crashing in. And the guns in the hands of the two players weren't the type that shot bullets. They were the type I'd seen before. One pull of the trigger and we'd be obliterated.

CHAPTER NINE

THEY MARCHED US into the night. Their guns reminding us this could be the day we die. In fact, I was sure this was our fate. Stuart Manning played cat and mouse with me so often there'd surely be a time he'd dispose of me and move on to the next toy. Perhaps Sage would be his new plaything. An attractive man with no social standing.

Capitalism masked as religion kept him captive. Sage's only diversion was sex. Not flirtation. Not romance.

Augmented reality games kept players in a suspended emotional state. Escape was delivered and controlled with erotic sensation from time to time. Just the right amount to keep them hooked, but not too much so their virgin minds could still cope. This far into the twenty-first century, Beta City had given in to full dominance.

But who was I to judge? I had sex with a harsh woman I hardly knew when I got here.

"The bottle neck is a sight to behold," said one of the game players. "But it's nothing like the canary-coloured stream that gives so much to so few."

I halted for a second, then kept walking so I wouldn't draw attention to myself. For the second time, I knew the voice behind the mask. *But how can it be?* I shook the thought out of my head.

We passed many buildings in need of repair. A decayed door here, a smashed window there. And the streets were getting even darker.

Sage scrunched his forehead, making it clear he had years of worry lines. "If I escape, man, you're dead to me."

"Really?" I replied. "Don't forget you saved me from these nutters. It was your choice to get involved."

"Hmm. Yeah. Well. Whatever."

There was a door at the side of a wooden house. One of them pulled a key from a pocket in his suit. He unlocked the door.

We followed him down a set of stairs as the other kept his gun locked on us from behind. It smelled like a public toilet down here, with a slight lemon scent. A meek attempt to freshen the place. Another door was at the bottom of the stairs. We huddled in front of it. He put the same key into the lock.

"Welcome, my friends," he said. Yep, I knew that voice.

He peeled off his mask. I was right. It was Carter.

"Where have you been?" My jaw stayed open in awe after I spoke.

"The gorilla is a welcoming creature," said the player

still masked. I knew that voice too.

"And he knows a great number of secrets," Carter replied, grinning.

It was Hudson. She peeled off her headpiece. I wasn't sure how to feel.

"It's okay, Tayler," Carter said. "Don't fear Hudson. You are both safe."

"But she handed me over to Stuart!" I panicked. "You can't trust her."

"Tayler, inside," she demanded. "Don't talk out here."

Carter opened the second door to reveal a huge modern kitchen. In front of it, a long wooden table, the type where monks would sit to break bread while keeping their vow of silence, took up most of the space. A middle-aged woman was stirring the contents of a fry pan on the stove. The sizzling garlic and onion was a welcome odour in contrast to the damp at the bottom of the stairs.

I turned to Hudson.

"We were offline when we brought you here," she explained.

"Really?"

She nodded. "Stuart is a madman. I was there when that player shot the dog."

"But you work for him. You know he does stuff like that."

"She didn't know," Carter said. "That was the first time an animal was killed for a game. I think he did it for your benefit. To scare you."

"You were one of them?" I asked Hudson. "How did you know it was actually a dog?"

"I disengaged my suit," she replied.

"Is that possible?" Sage asked.

"She knows how," Carter said. "That's why she's here with us."

"But I can't trust her." I was trembling. "She handed me over to Stuart! I could be dead now."

"Yeah, about that." Hudson unzipped part of her suit, pulled out her tobacco tin, and placed it on the table. "I have a lot of grovelling to do."

"You bet you have." I folded my arms rigidly to stop myself shaking.

Carter and Hudson gazed at each other, and Hudson shared a look of concern. But I still couldn't trust her. A harrowing roller coaster ride and a gelato splatter session were not my idea of a pleasant afternoon.

"He'd never kill you," she reasoned. "He has something else in mind. I'm not sure what, but he needs you alive. Shooting the dog was a way of scaring you to remind you he's in charge. But I've never seen him talk about anyone the way he talks about you."

"How so?" I asked.

"Like you're his bromance masturbation fantasy." She smirked.

"I don't trust you, Hudson. You could turn us all in at any moment."

"She won't," said Carter. "She saved me from Stuart. He was waiting at the train station when I got here. Then he kept me locked in an apartment. He gave me food and everything I wanted until Hudson rescued me. After the dog was shot, she knew he was a madman."

"You have the key to Stuart's apartment?" I asked her.

"He has an office in his apartment. With two separate

rooms. I worked in one, he in the other."

"Hold on," I said. "Carter, you must have been at Stuart's when I was there."

"Probably, but I was drugged most of the time."

The woman at the stove added chicken, grated parmesan, and something else to the mixture. I tasted the scent on my tongue, licking my lips and trying to swallow what wasn't there. She turned down the temperature and joined us.

"Where are your manners?" she asked. "I've been waiting for an introduction."

Carter introduced me and Sage to Sonya, their cook. She wore a cheeky smile and seemed affluent enough to dye her short hair white, giving off a mature-aged-student vibe with her thick rimmed glasses.

"What was that other ingredient?" I asked.

"Huh?" She looked at the fry pan.

"There was chicken and grated parmesan. What was the other thing you put in?"

"Chopped walnuts. We're having Aji de Gallina. Peruvian spicy creamed chicken." Sonya gestured to the long table. We sat.

She returned to the stove and added cream, I think. It came from a can. Maybe fresh cream was hard to come by here.

She let it simmer and before long, we were digging into a dish that was better than sex. Seriously. It was. Sage and I kept glancing at each other as if we'd never tasted food, often chuckling at how hungry we were.

Each bit of chicken had been chopped, amplifying the flavour as it slid on my tongue. Its velvety texture revealed samples of its spices, each combination conveying a unique succulent tang.

After our meal, I helped bring the dirty dishes back to the kitchen where a scrapbook of photos and handwritten recipes, all stuck down with sticky tape, lay open on the counter. Sonya sensed my curiosity.

"It's my great-great-grandmother's. And my most treasured possession."

"She's right," Carter said. "She treats that book better than a spouse."

"That's true." She pulled off her glasses. "I have a 'hands off' policy, Tayler. You so much as breathe on this book and I'll chop you up and baste you in Peri-peri sauce."

"As long as you serve me with a nice salad, I don't mind."

"Now, get out of my kitchen." She flipped a few pages to a dessert recipe. "You haven't finished eating yet."

Hudson moved to sit opposite me when I returned to the table. "Tayler, listen. I now understand how crazy Stuart is. I just thought he was eccentric before. I'd already disengaged my suit when we fetched you from Sage's building because...well, just because."

"No." I leaned forward. "I need all the facts if I'm to trust you."

"Okay. I had a hunch. A few things seemed fishy about Stuart for a while. He knew you were coming and—"

"How did he know I was coming to Beta City?"

"I'm not sure, but..."

"But what?" Carter asked.

"He talks to someone, sometimes."

"Who?" Sage asked.

Hudson opened her tobacco tin and took out her vaper.

"No smoking!" Sonya yelled. She held a large wooden spoon and flung it around like a weapon. "What have I said about lung-choking pollution at the dining table?"

"Sorry," Hudson called back. She rolled her eyes. "It's not wise to upset the woman who feeds you."

At least someone has the upper hand with Hudson.

"Who does Stuart talk to?" I asked.

"Someone with a robotic voice. I've never seen him, and I don't know where the voice comes from. They were talking before I knocked on his front door once, and another time before I exited."

"At his penthouse?" I asked.

She nodded. "This voice is who's really in charge of Beta City. I'm sure of it."

"How sure?" Carter asked.

"Stuart was preoccupied more than usual when he let me in. And the second time, he was freaking as he showed me out."

"He sounds like a fruit loop," Sage noted. "But how did he know Tayler or Carter were coming to Beta City?"

Hudson shrugged. "He told me where to meet Tayler."

"But how would he know?" Carter pondered. "And he also knew which train I'd be on when I got here. There he was, evil grin and all, waiting on the platform."

"Okay, I have no proof the voice is in charge," Hudson continued. "It's just a hunch, and only a hunch, but this disconnected voice knows a hell of a lot about you both."

"Which is why we're hiding down here," Carter reassured me.

"How did you end up working for Stuart?" I asked Hudson.

"I answered a job ad six months ago, and the rest is fate."

"How did you get to choose the job you wanted?" Sage's frustration was evident.

"She's not from Beta City," I replied.

"But how did you choose that job?" Sage asked again.

"I answered a job ad back home asking for public servants in Beta City. I had nothing better to do, so here I am."

"Hold on." Sage rubbed the back of his neck, over and over. "If that voice knows it all, it knows Tayler and Carter are down here."

"I told you before, I disengaged my gamer suit," Hudson replied. "I'm an expert hacker."

"She's created a secret off switch on our augmented reality suits." Carter pointed to the back of Hudson's thigh. Hudson pointed to a switch sewn into her suit. "Like we said before, when we rescued you, we weren't on the network."

I had butterflies in my stomach. "Your suits have cameras. I saw that dog streamed live on Hudson's computer through some blockhead's suit. Stuart can watch your video feed."

"Have you noticed our suits are a darker shade of grey than the others you've seen?" Hudson asked.

"Yes," I replied. "Sage's was the darkest."

"They're older suits," Sage replied. "My model never had a camera."

"Oh." I thought about it. "I noticed the camera on the other suit, but..."

"You're not convinced, are you, Tayler?" Carter studied me.

"Are you a hundred percent sure we can't be traced?"

"Pull out your device, Tayler," Hudson said.

"He doesn't have one," Carter replied. "He's been at Cradle Edge. Remember? The hippie town for organic life to thrive." He pulled out his device and placed it on the table. "Try it, Tayler."

I picked it up and gazed at the screen. The words "No Connection" spread in bold letters behind the glass.

"We don't have a signal down here." Hudson showed me her own device to prove her point. "We are in a solid concrete bunker. No internet connection. No Social Media Central."

"But Stuart can trace you to this building." Sage tapped his fingers on the table. "Your device would've worked until we got down here."

Hudson grinned. "No, Mr Paranoid. I ran a program on our devices to make Social Media Central cut out at certain spots."

"I'm still not convinced he won't find me." I lowered my head. "He'll work out what happened and come for me. Maybe that voice already knows I'm here."

"Not if I can help it." Hudson stared at her vaper tin as if it summoned her, glanced back at Sonya, then placed it inside her gamer suit.

I smelt cinnamon. Sonya poured a cup of sultanas, some butter, and some water into a saucepan and stirred.

"We're having sultana cinnamon loaf for dessert," Carter said. "With the creamiest butter you've ever tasted."

My stomach growled. Here I was, unconvinced Stuart wouldn't find us, and my tummy yearned for a treat, even though I just ate. I tried to recall the last time I tasted cinnamon. Some overly fatty doughnut back in Astra City, I thought. Sonya poured the sultana mixture into a small bowl, placed a tea towel under it, and put it in the fridge.

I kept watching Sonya cook until she was aware of my stare, so I studied our general space. The kitchen cabinets were fairly new, unlike the stove, oven, and fridge. And there were two more doors other than the entrance to this room.

"Whose place is this?" I asked.

"One of my lovers," Hudson said. "He usually rents it out, but I convinced him to let me have it for a couple of months."

"And that's all any of us need to know," Carter replied. "Anonymity is our friend."

"So, this is where the resurrection of the Life Experience Mob is going to be." I stood, imagining all the different scenarios we could recreate for the folk of Beta City. Then reality hit. "We're trapped down here." My butt hit my seat hard.

"You're right," Sage said. "I can't go to work tomorrow. I wasn't there today. I can't explain myself."

"I'm sorry." I gazed at his troubled face. "I've complicated your life."

"No, you didn't, man. I decided to help you. And looking at how things panned out, I'm okay with that."

"But your family won't be safe." I felt incredibly guilty.

"Not if the government thinks I'm missing," Sage explained. He reached for me.

"Collateral damage." I took his hand. "And what about you, Hudson?" I asked. "Once Stuart knows we're here, what will happen to the lover who owns this place?"

Hudson looked away, staring at nothing in particular.

Sonya stirred the refrigerated mixture in with the

ingredients waiting in another bowl. Soon, it was all in a tin and in the oven. Eventually, this place felt cosier, just through the magic of an aroma. The scent of cake baking gave calm. The perfect deceit for my sense of fear.

THAT EVENING, WE slept in a decent-sized room with mattresses on the floor. This communal bedroom was behind one of the doors. I still didn't know what was behind the other.

Carter opened several bottles of wine before bedtime. Hudson worked hard at winning me over, but, as I'd been deceived in the past by people who'd slept with me, my heart secured itself in barbed wire.

It was still dark when Sage pressed against me. He had his own mattress yet snuck onto mine. He kissed me. I pulled back. Then the reality of the danger we were in came back to me, so my lips met his.

Someone stirred. We stopped. No one seemed awake. Sage led me outside the bedroom. I carefully closed the door behind us.

He lay on the long wooden dining table and pulled me on top of him. His naked back hard against the wood. Here, where we'd drunk wine, eaten creamy chicken and sultana loaf, and indulged in spicy, savoury snacks with even more wine, we were to make love.

His arms embraced me while his legs firmly pressed me against him. Our warmest parts bonding between the flimsy layer of our cotton underwear. I was giving in to his invitation to form a union that could have any number of consequences. But I couldn't stop.

Stuart Manning had killed people due to his dangerous fascination with me. Tomorrow, I might be dead, or maimed. Or maybe Sage would be. I needed this. I yearned for this.

Our lips met again, and my illusion of refuge continued.

CHAPTER TEN

"YOU NEED TO understand, Tayler." Sage had the same tone as when he didn't want me to stay the night in his flat. "This was just sex."

"Are you comparing me to one of your pickups?"

I was confused. The previous night, *he* came on to *me*, yet I welcomed his change of heart. Life was too complex for this to be anything more than physical.

It was dark. I had no idea what time it was, or if day was breaking, as down here it was hard to tell. Gentle snores came from the bedroom, so I took a rough guess that morning was some time away.

"The cold makes this place smell damp."

Sage didn't respond. He just stared at me, his dark eyes judging me.

"So, *are* you comparing me to your hook-ups?" I stroked his cheek. I felt the need to share affection even if this was just sex. He didn't push my hand away.

"No, man, don't be stupid. A lot happened yesterday. My life can't go back to normal. I needed release. You understand. I need to stay sane. You didn't complain." He pressed my hand against his cheek. Mixed messages. "Hey, so what am I to you?"

"You're Sage. Someone I need to protect."

"Why?"

"I got you into this mess."

He turned, causing my hand to slip off his face. "No, man. I got *me* into this mess."

"But you blamed me yesterday. You said if you escape, I'm dead to you."

"Yeah, but..."

"You needed to escape your work life?"

"I don't know what I need." He had a suspicious glare. "Man, who hurt you?"

"Huh?"

"In love. Who's hurt you?"

Why does he want to know?

"I made amends with a famous blogger."

"So, no outstanding heartache?"

"Sage, is there a story you want to share? Is that why you radically changed the subject?"

"No, man. I keep my lovers at a distance."

"So they can't hurt you?"

"What are you guys doing up?" Carter shut the door behind him. "Oh. Don't answer. It's obvious."

"Comfort for comfort's sake," I replied.

While Carter and I grinned slyly at each other, Sage turned away.

"We need to find a way to safety," I said.

"If we had more than two augmented reality suits, we could all leave." Carter went to the pantry. "We could make our way to Cradle Edge, or somewhere else Stuart Manning has no control over." He returned with more of the spicy crackers we had the night before.

"Where did we get the suits we have?" I asked.

"Hudson was wearing one when she rescued me—"

"When the dog was shot," I said.

"When the dog was shot," Carter confirmed. "She had the insight to grab another which I quickly put on. Stuart had several of the old darker grey ones in a box. Hudson knew where they were."

"Why didn't you take..." I realised the answer to my own question. "You didn't take more because that would look suspicious. Two game players carrying extra suits."

"Could we"—Sage pointed at all three of us—"be hostages? Hudson wears the suit." He was cute when he was serious. He had the adorable smugness of a child proudly helping with the housework. "She could get us to the border." He took a cracker and crunched its edges.

"And what if more players joined them?" Carter said.

"We need to change the playing field." I stood. I thought if I paced, I'd come up with a solution. "Once Stuart loses control, he panics. Carter, we came here to start a revolution."

"No," they both exclaimed in unison.

"Now's not the time for revolution," Carter replied. "It's too risky."

"But you know as well as I do Stuart hates an uprising and..."

"And what, Tayler?" Sage frowned.

"And we'll be trapped forever down here if we don't do anything." I stopped pacing.

"What are you guys doing up?" Hudson gently closed the door behind her.

"Thinking of a plan to take control of Beta City," I replied. "And to sneak out unnoticed once chaos reigns."

"It's just too risky," Carter said.

"And what's the alternative?" Hudson asked. "None of us can stay here forever. Tayler's right."

Sage's sad dark eyes engaged me once more. "What about the Radical Faith Alliance?"

"What about it?" Hudson asked.

"My face is its logo," I replied.

"Why?" Carter asked.

I shrugged. "A plan to flush me out? People might take selfies with me or photograph me when I don't know it, to show their support for the movement. It will be easier for Stuart to find me once I'm posted all over Social Media Central."

"Why did he let you go in the first place?" Sage asked.

"Because, deep down, he likes Tayler." Carter looked as proud as a man finding that elusive word in a crossword puzzle. "Tayler challenges him. He gives Tayler a lifeline, then takes control again. Cat and mouse."

I rolled my eyes. "I know. Cat and mouse are our default settings. But let's get real here. It won't be cat and mouse forever. He nearly killed me several times."

"But he let you go during the Enemy Alien game,"

Hudson replied. "Trust me, you are his bromance."

"I know he has a weird fascination with me, but I'm not stupid enough to think he likes me."

Hudson and Carter exchanged glances as if a secret message was passed between them through telepathy.

"No. Seriously. He'll come for me because he knows I'm alive, regardless of getting me to run from those grey-clad dorks." I growled in frustration, then shut my eyes for calm. "Now listen, we have to start a revolution. My revolution. Maybe it's our revolution. Whatever it is, The Radical Faith Alliance must have influence while we stay hidden. We must work out what Stuart's plan is and take control."

"Yeah. I get it. Take control of the narrative." Hudson stood and paced, reaching for her vaper in the pocket of her pyjama pants at the same time.

"You said Stuart makes his plans up as he goes along," Sage confirmed.

"We can't do this," Carter said. "It's too risky."

"But Tayler's right." Hudson exhaled a long steady stream of smoke. "I've worked for Stuart long enough to know he has no clue what to do with Tayler once he's caught." She stared blankly towards our communal bedroom. We looked back too. There was nothing to see. "Tayler, have you slept with Stuart?"

"Why would I sleep with a sociopath?"

She paused to take a longer puff. "He dresses well. He has a cultured voice."

"Have you got the hots for him?" I asked.

She grimaced. "He's too much like my dad."

Her tobacco had that sweet smell I remembered. It wasn't marijuana. It was candy-like with hints of strawberry and apple.

"Stuart is just a silly politician," Hudson continued. "No plan but happy to take praise even if it's unwarranted. And he's not in charge anyway."

"That robotic voice is," I confirmed.

"Who is it?" Sage asked.

"Maybe it's The World Bank," I replied. "That's who controlled him in Astra City. And hey, this is a city of slave workers. Low paid..."

Sage nodded.

"...and brainwashed through a made-up religion. So, we'll create a local movement that will make living to work *so yesterday*. And it already has a counter manifesto. Half our work is done. Oh, hold on. We're in a bunker with no internet. And if we step out—"

"Wait." Hudson seized her device from the kitchen. "The Radical Faith Alliance, you said?" We nodded. She meandered upstairs and out through the front door.

"What is she smoking?" Carter asked.

"I want a puff." Sage smirked.

"It's not dope," I said. "But it has the same effect for a brief time. Then she snaps out of it."

"I like this version of her," said Carter. "We have to encourage her to vape more."

"Let's all puff." Sage grinned.

"Oh. Yes. Please." Carter mimed vaping, then wobbled his head, crossed his eyes, and let his tongue hang out.

"I'll abstain and let her have it all," I said. "I cope better with tranquil Hudson around."

She soon returned. Her vaper was back in her pocket. "A right to ambition. A right to status. A right to dream. I have an idea, but first, I need to know what happened between you and Stuart in Astra City?"

I reminded her about my rise to fame by partying with famous social media influencers. The same social media influencers who were financed by Stuart to sneak political messages into their posts. Carter mentioned his Life Experience Mob who brought real-life experiences from the past to the people of Astra City. Hudson realised that, together, we helped the citizens turn away from Social Media Central and communicate face to face, taking influence away from Stuart. I added the bit about the secret bunker housed with people set up in movie-style studios to look like the living rooms of the fake characters they had to represent in order to further influence those they spoke to through webcam.

"Okay, let me get this straight." Hudson stroked her forehead as if rubbing away a headache. "Stuart was in control but lost it when folk were no longer addicted to their screens."

I nodded. "So, to do the same thing here, we have to wean them off Enemy Alien."

"We only play it to numb the pain of long hours and mindless work." Sage paused and read our faces. "The Life Experience Mob revamped as the Radical Faith Alliance will shake this city up. This Stuart dude will lose his shit."

"These nutters will stop running around in augmented reality suits, using the internet to relay where I am." I danced on the spot.

"But then he'll target Sage's loved ones," Carter said.

"We don't have another plan." Sage chuckled for some reason. "Look. I was at dinner last night. I've never sat at dinner with others. I didn't say much, but I kept thinking *I want to learn to cook.* And, man, being here with you peeps made me feel so connected I needed a *special* cuddle in the middle of the night." He grinned at me. It felt nice. "And if we get the word out to get peeps cooking for friends at home, man, we can change what Beta City is all about."

"Convoluted," Carter supposed. "But I guess we can't do nothing."

"I'm glad you're all seeing it my way." I danced again.

"And this all has to hinge on Tayler," Hudson explained. "Sage will have to stay hidden so his loved ones and Stuart and whoever Sage's boss is will just think we're missing."

Hudson strolled to the kitchen and pulled out a large piece of paper from the bottom drawer. We helped her spread it over the dining table. "We are devising a media plan. Tayler, you and I are going to sneak out dressed in the game suits. We'll visit my friend, Vanessa, a multimedia artist, where we'll shoot a series of videos in which you will instigate topics of conversation for upcoming dinner parties. Esoteric topics. Existential topics. Everyday topics. Like how people feel about their parents picking a boss to enslave them while they're still in the womb. How they can find ways to rise up against this oppressive system and find a new normal. Hell, anything to get them thinking and talking."

"Use the mantra Stuart is using for the Radical Faith Alliance's message against him." I squealed in delight. The sound even surprised me. "But how will the Enemy Alien players get involved if they live in an alternate reality?' I tapped my chin. "They need to peel off their suits and throw them away for good. They need to eat dinner with people, like Sage said, not scare the city's citizens."

"Are we sure we want to do this?" Sage asked.

"You seemed pretty excited about it a moment ago," Hudson replied. "It's either that or live down here for the rest of our lives."

And so, our plan was born. We mapped out *my* revolution. We'd upload a daily video with a conversational topic that would move our uprising further. And before Stuart could come up with another ill-thought-out plan, we'd walk away from Beta City still true to Carter's original reason for coming here.

Several hours later, Hudson photographed the large piece of paper with our media campaign for posterity, then, after we took a short nap to make up for the sleep we lost, she got into one of the suits. I wore the other.

With her device and our ridiculous outfits disconnected from the all-knowing Social Media Central, we departed to see Vanessa.

"A cardboard landing is preferred to a fabric one."

The player who spoke walked by my side.

"But doesn't fare well in spin cycle."

Another joined Hudson. She faced me, and instantly, I knew I had to reach down and click my connect switch. She did the same. If our suits weren't turned on, these gamers would be suspicious.

CHAPTER ELEVEN

THE SKY WAS amazing. I'm not sure which level of the game we entered, but I assumed we were playing in line with our new companions. A small shiny spaceship zoomed past, and I could hear its propulsion. I never heard a jet engine of any kind until this moment.

And there was a whole universe of colours I never encountered the last time I wore one of these suits. The heavens were splashed with paint, forever swirling behind a mass of stars. The mothership floated on the horizon, dark and foreboding, making itself the centrepiece of this reimagined landscape.

Now and again, a being would pass, mumbling something while sounding like a talking tuba with limited vocabulary. I knew they were ordinary humans, not gamers, but in this augmented reality world, they strolled around on four tentacles. Saliva dripped from their mouths and made a squelch as it wet the ground. Their acned skin glistened, reflecting the palette of the sky.

Nearby dwellings had morphed into corrugated iron shacks, all in need of repair. And while I could feel the concrete under my shoes, I saw muddy paths where footprints were left by Hudson and our friends as I followed.

"The caretaker is making its presence felt," said one player.

"Will the caretaker shoot its death ray?" the other responded.

"At what?" Hudson asked. She gasped.

Why did she speak? Stuart will recognise her voice through the network.

"No," the player replied. "At the Enemy Alien, if it sees him before we do." The gamer pointed to the large spacecraft.

Ah. The Caretaker is the mothership!

"We've been called to another mission," Hudson said, with a weird raspy voice.

"Where are we going?" the first player asked.

"You can't come with us." Her voice was deeper and creepier.

"You'll need safe passage." The first player halted. "We will protect you from the Caretaker. It may mistake you for the Enemy Alien."

"How?" I froze on the spot. *It was just one word. But I shouldn't have spoken. How good can those speech algorithms be?*

"The Caretaker's captain has been known to drink,"

Player Two said. "In his fevered state, he hears the hyena."

Hudson and I waited for further clarification. When it didn't come, she didn't ask. Shame though. Her strange vocal tone was comic relief to the doubt playing on my mind.

"My friend and I must go alone," she finally said. She crossed her arms. "Read my signal."

"Is that the signal of the snake charmer before she dances?" Player One asked.

"No," the second gamer replied. "It's the universal sign for help. We must follow this team to provide safe passage."

"It's not the universal sign for help," her croaky voice said. "It's the sign of a secret mission."

"Are you capturing the hyena?" the second gamer asked. "If so, you'll need our protection."

Were these lunatics tipped off?

Hudson said nothing and kept walking. I followed with our two unwanted friends trailing close behind. More inane phrases left their lips while I eased my concerns by losing myself in this make-believe reality.

We arrived at a crystal structure with sharp edges pointing to the sky. I concluded the rays it emitted from various points emerged from where its windows were. Hudson stood at a triangular entrance with no door, yet she pressed an imposing button on its frame.

She told the players to keep watch from a distance in a less raspy, more sing-song manner. She reached down and turned off her suit. I did the same.

A voice spoke through a speaker. Hudson replied with one word: "Edelweiss."

Hudson and I entered the building. With our suits switched off, I could clearly see golden metallic doors slide shut behind us on an entrance that was rectangular, not tri-angular. We took off our masks.

"For heaven's sake." I shook my head. "Why did those weirdos join us?"

"What do you mean? Is that a *tone* I detect?"

Hudson was right. An accusation was clear in my voice.

"Say what you need to say, Tayler."

"You've sold me out before. How do I know you had nothing to do with those gamers?" I pointed at the elevator in front of us. "How do I know Vanessa is real and Stuart Manning isn't waiting up there to bonsai me? Or plant me among the edelweiss?"

She regarded me like a serial killer deciding on whether to let me live.

"Hudson, I'm serious. You've fooled Carter. You fooled me to an extent, but really, why should I trust you?"

"Who else would put on a weird voice to throw those loonies off our scent?"

"But maybe that's part of the act. 'Tayler, Carter asked me to meet you.' And the next thing I know I'm handed over to Stuart. How do I know he's not up there now?"

"Stand right where you are, Tayler. No, I'm serious. Don't move."

She stepped outside and contacted Vanessa again. I lis-tened to them banter as Hudson pretended we hadn't made it inside yet. She was buzzed in again, then gave me a look of victory.

"That doesn't prove anything," I said. "Vanessa could be working for Stuart."

"Tayler, these are your choices. Come with me, meet Vanessa, and start our revolution. Or be stuck in Beta City forever, running from dorks who concern themselves with the hyena's mirth, the caretaker's death ray, or whatever loony musings you'll need to talk about every time they show up."

I grunted like something prehistoric. "You're stepping into the elevator first. In fact, we're holding hands so I can pull you in as a human shield if Stuart's there."

Hudson chuckled. "Oh, Tayler. I'm going to be your bargaining chip? Sweetheart, I have street cred. You have influencer experience—"

"I *have* street cred."

"Running around with social media socialites? Finding people to make love to in Cradle Edge? Bedding me like the gentle marshmallow you are."

"Well, you showed *no* affection."

"It's called taking control, Tayler. Fulfilling my needs. Like you and Sage did this morning."

The elevator doors opened. She entered. I reluctantly followed.

"TAYLER, ACCEPT IT. Whether you want to or not, you need to put your faith in me. I can protect you. I know what we're up against. I've worked with your nemesis, and although I thought he was kooky, the day that dog died..."

The elevator stopped.

"I'm a marshmallow lover?"

Hudson ignored me. She entered a code on a numerical panel to the side. The lift opened. An older woman with wavy long hair and wire-framed spectacles greeted us.

Stuart wasn't in sight.

"Tayler, this is Vanessa. Vanessa, Tayler."

We entered her apartment.

"Nice to meet you," I said.

Clutter was her choice of décor. I hit my head on something hanging from the ceiling. It made other things clank and clatter. Little model cars. Cutlery moulded into human shapes. Decorative pieces of coloured glass. I lowered my head and strolled towards our host.

A modest kitchen was to my right, while a white antique bed next to an open hanger with a range of men's shirts was against the wall to my left. I quickly realised the pinstriped shirt Vanessa wore was not designed for a woman. The buttons were on the wrong side.

Behind her was a device set up on a tripod with a couple of lights to its side. The back wall was painted light grey. An ideal shade to stand in front of and vlog from.

"The perfect studio for you to record special messages from," Hudson said to me.

"I was thinking the same thing," I replied.

I touched the shirts. There were enough to make it look as if my videos were shot on different days. This stage of the plan felt legit.

"Satisfied?" Hudson asked.

"As these videos are posted, we can sneak out of Beta City before the final vlog goes public." My anxiety was disappearing.

"What's he talking about, Hudson?"

"We need your help," she replied. "But first, can we stay the night? Two Enemy Alien losers followed us. They're waiting outside your building."

"They'll leave soon," Vanessa supposed. "They have shorter attention spans than my followers." She pointed at a small round dining table. We sat. "Now, why are you here?"

Hudson showed her the picture of our media plan. Thirty days of short video messages where I would engage gamers to join the Radical Faith Alliance, peel off their augmented reality suits, and cook for their friends. Some vlogs would contain recipes Sonya wrote down for us in an easy-to-follow way. Other posts would contain conversation starters. Eventually, we'd take the slogans Stuart had planted and use them for a city-wide workers' strike.

"So, let me get this straight." Vanessa stood and wandered to a set of drawers near her bed. "You want these messages uploaded daily so you can escape before the last one is posted. Who's going to upload?"

Hudson gave Vanessa a cutesy look. "Edelweiss, we were hoping the last week of vlogs would be—"

"No." Vanessa pulled at a drawer. "I have a better idea."

"Edelweiss?" I whispered.

"Shush," Hudson replied.

Vanessa pulled the drawer right out, came over, and dropped it on the table. It was filled with old devices. There were at least thirty. Recently, Astra City turned off the telephony network leaving these devices to only work with the all-knowing Social Media Central. Or the Alta Net if you had someone who knew how to hack these things so you could read the hidden historical truth of the world.

Vanessa fished out one of the older models. "I'll get my friends to post one of your vlogs each day from a different device. Then they'll turn off that device and destroy it. With uploads coming from different places around Beta City,

Stuart won't have a clue where you're hiding. You'll confuse the old goat, no end."

"Why have you got so many devices?" I picked up one that was similar to a model I owned a while back. Its glass was smudged with fingerprints.

"Tayler, I'm an old media whore. I was vlogging when you were being toilet trained. And each one of these is part of my journey. They're my friends. They're as important as the thousands who visit my channel to hear my musings on melon ballers, burnt toast, or my latest fart."

"But you're willing to destroy your devices for our cause." I glanced at Hudson who didn't react.

Vanessa nodded. "Honey, I've seen the world change. Or at least my corner of it. First, we used to get private messages through Social Media Central warning us who we could speak to and who we shouldn't contact. Soon, we realised when one of our friends, and dear, all our friends are online...so we realised when one of our friends didn't reply to a message, we were on their blacklist. The Government deemed our relationship invalid. That was Stage One.

"Then our algorithms were tampered with so we stayed in touch with whoever the Government considered valid every time we logged on to Social Media Central. The friends we saw on our feed were approved of, but if they were no longer there, the Government didn't want us to connect with them anymore. That was Stage Two.

"Stage Three is coming. I know it. I don't know if this silly Enemy Alien game is part of it or if there'll be another way the Government approves who we talk to and who fades from our lives."

"We have Social Media Central, too, back in Astra City,"

I said. "But it is used differently."

Hudson tried to bring one of the devices back to life. "The lesson here is, no matter where you are, Social Media Central is being used to control the masses."

"I'm stating the obvious but..." Vanessa snorted in frustration. "Tayler, the history I've been told through life has changed. What I remember as a child, some of it taught to me at a school by teachers, has been revised over my lifetime." She blew out of the side of her mouth with the same vexation. "A very long time ago, two towers were destroyed in a place called New York."

"You mean, two towers, several skyscrapers, and the large statue of a woman with a crown." Hudson looked at me, content she clarified our host's story.

"No." Vanessa moaned. "I was very young when it happened. I watched it on a thing we called a TV. I remember clearly the chaos in a few places across America, but in New York the focus was the fall of two towers."

"They were internet towers," Hudson added.

"No. They were towering skyscrapers used for business purposes. The statue of that woman didn't tumble. Residential towers weren't attacked. But I clearly remember two planes flew into these towers."

"Planes?" I smirked.

"Vanessa, you were just a child. You imagined they were planes."

"No. No. No. Listen to me. History is rewritten, reimagined, or forgotten. This incident, which sent shock waves around the world, was known by everybody until Social Media Central reorganised our thinking." She marched up to me. "Tayler, is there any way to see the Alta Net here in Beta

City?"

"I don't know. My friend Carter would know."

"Tayler said we all have a different historical reality..." Hudson paused, digesting her friend's alternative take of the event. "I mean, if SMC is different here to what it is where you're from, Tayler, then I doubt another social network's transmissions would reach here from Astra City." She pulled out her tobacco tin. "Are you sure no residential towers were hit?"

Vanessa looked as defiant as a general winning a battle. "See, the authorities play with the truth. Trust me, I was alive when it happened. That's why your Radical Faith Alliance plan is a clever idea. It's what we need right now. Overthrow the status quo. Overthrow Stuart. Once we rid ourselves of that weedy guy and Social Media Central, Entrepreneurship, those Enemy Alien failures, and the whole effing system, we will breathe." She examined several devices from the drawer. "And these agents of fiction will be something the next generation will never endure."

I saw the irony in her life of vlogging adding to the noise of SMC, but we were there to start a revolution. My old influencer friends were just as guilty when they found they had fans. So was I.

We started scripting.

WHEN MY FIRST videos went live, many asked what certain cooking terms meant in the comment field. Julienne was the one that confused most people. It was too dangerous for me to use a device and reply. Fortunately, other citizens came on board and explained these terms.

By the end of the week, people asked about the Radical Faith Alliance's manifesto. Some questioned how they could have ambition when they were slaves to a system. And while they knew they had a right to dream, some asked "why bother?" Others who shared their dreams encouraged the non-believers.

Ten days later, the seeds we planted had not only taken root, they thrived like weeds. Many Enemy Alien gameplayers left their augmented reality outfits in the closet. They mastered Sonya's, or rather her great-great-grandmother's, recipes. Our followers invited friends over to sample what they'd cooked, drink wine, and reimagine a society where they could depend on each other, rather than work to survive. And they were encouraged to invite an elder to their dinner table. Someone who could relay memories that contradicted history as told by Social Media Central.

Some diehard players still donned their figure-hugging anti-reality suits, but with so few, they stood out in a crowd either going to, or coming home from, a dinner party.

I stayed hidden in the bunker. I couldn't afford to be recognised with Stuart Manning waiting for me in that born-again city.

Two weeks into our campaign, we celebrated our success. We all helped Sonya create a feast, and when she had to stir a simmering pot, she instructed us on whether to slice or cut into small cubes, to grate or chop finely, or to season with salt and pepper or some exotic spice.

The man who lent Hudson this shelter had a home delivery service with a grocery store in town, which was why we ate so well. Sonya had the password and would step outside with her shopping list and order as quickly as possible. I don't know who paid for the food, which made me suspect Stuart may have set this up with Hudson, and we were sitting ducks. But then she'd do something that made me feel I was overthinking.

And this was the silly part. I could have asked whose money we were spending, but from time to time, even with the success of our revolution, I still expected Stuart and his gamer stormtroopers to bash down the doors and take us. So, I had this weird logic. If I didn't ask who paid the bills, I wouldn't get a vague answer that would only worry me more.

Hudson donned her augmented reality suit to pick up champagne for our party. Carter was tempted to invite a couple of guests from our growing list of followers. I was adamant it was too early for anyone to know where we were. I suggested a larger farewell party the following week. One where I'd make my escape, even though as yet I didn't know how.

There was that fruity fragrance again. Carter and Hudson were vaping in the kitchen. Their freshly blended pesto with spaghetti was being chomped between puffs, laughter, and serious conversation. At least it looked serious. Eyebrows were scrunched and seedy glances exchanged. It seemed Carter was the "chosen one". The only person allowed to indulge in Hudson's unconventional blend.

Sonya, Sage, and I ate at the table.

"Come clean," I said to Sonya after several glasses of champagne and not enough bruschetta to soak up my merriment. "You've avoided my question several times."

She chuckled. "I worked for your nemesis, Tayler."

"You worked for Stuart Manning? No! Really?"

She nodded. "Breakfast and dinner seven days a week for the past year. I begged for time off. He finally said yes. I should have returned by now."

"Hold on. If you worked for Stuart, you would have met Hudson."

She nodded. "She was the one who suggested I leave."

"When the dog was shot?"

"When the dog was shot."

I exhaled, surprising myself at how much relief blew away with that breath.

"So, you trust Hudson?" Oddly, I felt coy asking.

"She was led by short-sighted ambition before she woke up to Stuart's madness. Don't worry, Tayler. She has your back."

"Why did you work for him?"

"It's Beta City. It's a tough place to find a good job. And even tougher to stay in work. And the money was good. Hell, we had government jobs."

"But you haven't been to work for a while. Aren't you scared of what he'll do to your family?"

Sage reached for my hand from the opposite side of the table. "Tayler, if we're missing, nothing happens until someone proves we're hiding. I've told you that."

"But we're talking about Stuart Manning," I replied. "A cold-hearted murderer. I know what he can do. He won't wait for confirmation."

"It's okay," Sonya replied. "None of my family are in Beta City."

"So, where are they?" I asked.

She took a steady sip, placed her glass down, and rested

her hands on the table.

"My family live in a town where Social Media Central has a stronger hold than here. My husband and sons were addicted to their screens. They never realised I was gone when I'd take long walks to clear my sense of isolation. I'd talk and they'd grunt or give one-word answers, which had nothing to do with what I asked. So, I started staying at a friend's place." A wry smile came to her lips. "I'd come home after a night away, and my witless family had no idea I wasn't there the night before. Then I stayed two, then three nights. They didn't miss me. I lived with strangers. My sons were no longer the citizens I raised, and my husband, well, he was not the man I married."

"But if you weren't in bed with your husband, he would know." Sage twirled his finger in his hair.

Sonya shook her head. "He wasn't connected to reality anymore. I could be murdered in bed with my blood soaking the sheets and he'd still stare at his screen until the smell of my rotting corpse made him notice me. Then, instead of disposing of me, he would have slept in the guest bedroom."

We chuckled.

"Actually, he did notice me when it mattered," she continued. "And it mattered when he watched porn."

I nearly chuckled.

"What made you choose Beta City?" I asked.

"A new life, and like you, Tayler, I didn't know much about this place. But it was a city. An anonymous place to start again. Then I met Stuart. He romanced me. And then..." Sonya lowered her head as if she'd just heard of the death of a friend. "Then I saw his true colours."

"Who was the lover you had back home?" Sage asked.

"The one you saw when you didn't come home for days."

"Rosemary. We talked about our starvation for human contact, then we gave in to our feelings. I'd go home feeling guilty. I was so stupid at first. No one at home noticed my guilt, or the way my feet glided on air when my guilt passed."

With one hand still on mine, Sage reached for Sonya's. I did the same. She reciprocated. An intimate triangle at one end of the dining table.

"What made Rosemary special?" I asked.

"The simple fact she wasn't an SMC zombie. She observed what was going on and used something my family no longer had."

Sage and I waited for her to continue. Eventually, Sage asked.

"Critical thinking," Sonya replied. "The lost art of observing what's going on and using your own wisdom and experience to analyse your world."

"Instead of being told what to think," I added.

"And thinking opinion is fact." Sage stared down the end of the table. I wondered what he was thinking. He fixed his absent gaze on me. "What made your woman special?"

"Are you asking me or your boyfriend?" Sonya chuckled. "It was her mind, Sage. Her mind was sexy."

"Huh?" He snapped out of his headspace.

"Like I said before, Frank and I still, you know, bisected my triangle, but it became pornographically mechanical. Like he was having sex with a blow-up doll. So, I imagined *his* air-filled erection to bounce up and down on, picturing a room of hot men just to get off. One to my right. One to my left—"

"And one to go wee wee wee all the way home." Sage

smirked at his own dad-joke. "But your woman. Rosemary. What made her the one?"

"Our romantic evenings always began with a board game, a bottle of wine, and old jazz records. And trust me, Sage, that's the type of date you and Tayler need to have. It leads to sharing stories and sharing ideas. And to sharing love. For if you don't know someone's mind, you don't know who you're lovin'."

Sage's eyebrows scrunched together like tie-dyed cloth. Sonya winked at him. But I was also questioning my own sexual behaviour. My apparent marshmallow approach with Hudson. My "what exactly is my deal with Sage?" confusion.

"Next week is all about extending networks." Hudson's voice took my attention. The screwy tobacco had worn off. "Tayler encourages people to look at the comments people have left under the vlogs and invite someone to dinner outside their neighbourhood."

"That's good," Carter replied. "The middle class will cook for the poor. Others from the middle class will visit the slums for the first time in their lives. We need to cross-pollinate the people."

"What about the rich?" Sage asked.

"I encourage them to participate," I replied. "But who knows what the people who keep Entrepreneurship alive will do."

"They'll make their cooks cater for people they know," said Sonya. "The riff-raff will never enter their sanctuaries."

Hudson and Sage nodded and joined us at the table.

"I use Stuart's slogans," I continued. "I tell everyone to be ambitious. To dream. And by the end of the week, I encourage all workers to go on strike."

"No one will strike," Sage said. "Their families will suffer."

"Entrepreneurship needs to be shaken somehow," Carter replied.

"An easy thing to say when you don't live here." Sage left the table.

I followed him.

"We have to contact some Radical Faith Alliance followers before the end of next week," Carter explained. "We'll talk to them face to face. Get them to be part of our escape plan." He caught my eye as I stood at the bedroom door. "Then we'll use them to keep their eyes open in Beta City when me, Tayler, and any of you, escape."

Sonya gasped. "Are you high?"

"You really have no idea how risky that is," Sage yelled from the bedroom. He stared at me like a sky diver whose parachute didn't open.

"How are we escaping?" Hudson asked.

Carter beamed. "I've got something in the pipeline. Maybe without the help of our followers."

I shut the door behind me. I was relieved Carter had a plan, preferably without anyone else's help.

"Come with me." I joined Sage on the mattress. "Come with me to Cradle Edge. You said as long as you're missing, your family is safe."

"And then what?" he asked.

"And then you'll have freedom and peace of mind."

"And I'll never see my family again."

"How often do you see them now?"

"Tayler!"

"No, seriously. Are you close?"

"That's not the point, man."

I longed to caress his back but was worried he'd see it as a cheap ploy for sex, rather than an act of love from a friend.

"Sage, I haven't seen my parents for a long time. They love taking selfies more than they love me."

"You said Social Media Central ain't important in Astra City anymore. You could see your folks. Man, you could have a better relationship with your mum and dad than I have with mine, yet you don't bother."

"What stopped you from seeing *your* family?" I knew the answer before he said it.

"Work."

"But you found time to play Enemy Alien. Why couldn't you see them instead?"

Sage mumbled like a politician caught out.

"Escape with me," I said. "Help me find my estranged parents. Let's get to know them."

"Are you asking as a lover or a friend?"

"As a fr—"

He came closer. "As a...?" He kissed my cheek. "Friend, you say?" He kissed me again. "Hudson's a friend. Carter's a friend. They're coming too?" He gave me a peck on the lips.

"Sage, I don't know what Carter's escape plan is. But I want you with me."

"As a friend? Or as your lover? Your boyfriend? Your darling? Sweetheart?"

A longer kiss to my lips.

"Well, man. What's your answer?"

A long, lingering kiss. Then he stood, fondled my un-shaven chin, and left the bedroom. My heart floated into the clouds, but my head forced me to recall my lack of successful relationships.

My mind eventually stopped ticking, so I re-joined the dinner party. It wasn't long before Sage and I put our cards on the table.

CHAPTER TWELVE

"WHAT IS THIS?" Sage asked me.

"You tell me."

We just had sex in the middle of the night again.

"No, seriously," I said. "I'm balancing on a tightrope."

"Bad comparison, man."

"But an apt one. What are you scared of?"

His jaw clasped shut. Nothing was said for a while. His silence was irritating.

"Okay then," I began. "Let *me* start. I have trust issues. And I sense you have too."

"Guilty as charged."

Sage jumped down from the kitchen counter and grabbed his boxers from the floor. We dressed. Our sleepwear sponged all fluid from our skin. He gestured to the dining table. We sat.

"Who's the fashion blogger you told me about?" he asked.

"A sassy redhead who brought me out of my lonely shell and showed me..." I didn't expect this to be a difficult conversation. "She showed me fame. I got hooked. Then she betrayed me."

"Another man?"

I nodded. Then, to avoid talking about it, I got up, grabbed some disinfectant, and sprayed the benchtop instead.

"A guy named Jett hurt me," Sage confessed. I returned to the table with rag still in hand. "Just before I was a gamer, I met Jett. He moved in. He kept me sane."

"What was he like?"

"Weird slick hairstyle. Always dressed in black. Wore short-sleeved shirts even when it was cold, but never wore shorts. Go figure? Affectionate as a puppy."

"What did he do for a living?"

"He wasn't from Beta City. Just passing through."

"And he left?"

"Four months of arguments and make-up sex. Four months of talking about our future. Four months of all the shit that comes at the start of a relationship."

"And he left."

"He wanted me to come with him. I told him I couldn't over and over. My family would be in danger."

"But if your boss thought you were missing..."

"He wasn't private. He put our relationship status on SMC. We were public."

"Then he left."

"Then he left. We had a big argument about leaving Beta City. I went to bed. He packed and left."

"Didn't he say goodbye?"

"Nope. Not even a note. I got up as soon as I heard the door slam to check for one. No goodbye. No note."

Sage's eyes had a misty sheen.

"Did you cry?" I asked.

"Not then. But since..." He nodded. "From time to time, I cry, but gaming stopped me caring." He looked away. "How did you deal with your girlfriend leaving?"

"See, that's the thing. She was already with someone else. I didn't know."

He waited for me to continue. But I was processing. Madi and I worked out our differences. Yet here I was with someone I felt something for, unable to put it behind me.

Sage grabbed my wrist as I stood. "Don't walk away," he said. "You know about Jett. Tell me about Madeline Q."

"We met because Stuart Manning planned it that way. He was the other man, but she was the person who brought me to danger."

"What? That's just weird."

"She recruited me, making me a social influencer. I joined her friends to sway public opinion to whatever Stuart wanted the masses to think."

"What happened next?"

"Madi and I were captured and brought to Stuart. That's when I learned it had all been staged. I escaped, eventually. But I was betrayed into thinking we had something. And we did. But she still went through with Stuart's plan until we, and her influencer friends, were in danger.

"You should have seen her crumble when her social

media was taken over by Stuart. Then she was accused of murdering someone who wasn't dead. When Stuart realised the victim was still alive, he had her killed." I felt nauseous. "Madi and I have been through a lot of serious stuff, which is why we're still friends."

"Friends with benefits?"

I nodded.

Sage wrapped his arms around me. "I cried alone, even when I thought I was over him." He let go of me and wandered back towards our collective sleeping quarters.

"Sage?"

"Shh. You'll wake everybody."

"You have more to tell me."

"To be continued."

"Are you upset because I'm leaving Beta City?"

He shut the door behind him. And that was it. I was Jett. The man who left. Except this time, he had the rest of the week to stay mad at the person responsible.

Over the next few days, I kept asking Sage to escape with me, but his answer was always no. And more and more, I feared losing him.

CHAPTER THIRTEEN

IT TOOK MOST of the week to convince Carter it was a bad idea to invite anyone we didn't know personally to our farewell dinner. Just because we had loyal Radical Faith followers did not mean we could risk seating these acquaintances at our dining table. He agreed to a compromise. We invited Vanessa instead.

Again, Sonya prepared more food than we could eat. But we were thriving on nervous energy. Understatement was not the order of the day.

I mastered the art of cooking steak, a skill I never expected to learn. With Sonya watching over my shoulder, she made sure each piece was flame grilled for the right amount of time. Its crispy odour was enough to give me a phantom iron hit.

Sonya taught Carter how to make mushroom sauce. I had to taste. The earthy tang of delectable fungi took me to heaven. *How will I cope without Sonya's talents?*

Vanessa brought a few bottles of wine she'd been keeping for a special occasion, but was disappointed only Sonya helped her drink it. Carter demanded we keep a clear head for our night-time escape. Alcohol was too risky. Hudson, Carter, and I drank sparkling water instead. So did Sage, even though he wasn't fleeing with us.

Hudson was, however, vaping her mysterious tobacco. Her stress levels were high, and with Sonya a wee bit tipsy, she got away with smoking at the dinner table. And to stop Carter admonishing her for dulling her senses, Hudson offered him a puff. His need to calm down overrode his caution. Lightheaded Carter was in the house.

With enough grub to feed an army, we sat down to our meal. The first topic of conversation was sparked by something we were all curious about earlier that day.

"How come you don't work?" Sage asked Vanessa.

He blurted this out with no preamble, but we were glad he did.

Vanessa quickly chewed the mouthful of steak she just popped in her mouth. "I've had sponsors from way back, funding my vlogs. My authenticity comes down to mentioning Organic Harvest Toasted Muesli at the end of my videos. Or having a carefully placed can of Carmichael's Creamed Corn somewhere in shot." She plunged her knife into her meat and cut. "Honey, I sold out generations ago. But if I hadn't, I'd be a slave to some filthy rich ninny, making their dreams come true while mine were never realised."

Sage applauded, then Hudson, then the rest of us.

Vanessa stood and bowed before returning to a piece of rib eye she'd just sliced.

"Did you ever take your brand beyond the vlogs?" I asked.

Again, Vanessa chomped fast. "What do you mean?"

"There was a video I watched about a wealthy couple—"

"*Maze and Mazda and Friends*," Hudson interrupted.

"No. It wasn't them."

"*The Petersons*," Vanessa suggested.

I shook my head.

"Was it Edward and Maryanne?" Sonya asked.

"I think so. Is that the one where they have a friend who claims to be rich, yet we never see evidence of her wealth?"

Sonya nodded. "It's called *My Perfect Life*. You find it through the Reality Wars app."

"They were the first family with too much money to make a reality show about their lives on SMC," said Vanessa. "I love the drunk one. What's her name?"

"Frances," Sonya replied. "Her and Peter got it on in the latest episode."

"Peter? Really?" Vanessa stared into space. "I thought he was gay."

"Maybe he's bi," I said.

"Well, if he is, he's coming out late." Vanessa topped her wine glass to its brim. "I've watched that shit religiously since the first upload, and I've never seen Peter make a move on a woman."

"He did in yesterday's upload." Sonya waved her glass in front of Vanessa. It was promptly filled.

"Isn't it dangerous to pop outside this bunker and watch

that show?" I weighed up any holes in tonight's escape. "Stu-art Manning knows who you are."

"I gave her an unregistered device," Carter said. He studied his fingernails. "I should have cut these."

"How can a device be unregistered?" Hudson asked, blowing smoke from the side of her lips. "And your finger-nails are fine."

"Really?" Carter scratched his upper back. "Yeah, I guess long nails come in handy. I can graze anyone who foils our escape."

Sage curled one of his ringlets tight around his finger. I breathed in Hudson's cloudy exhale. I ignored its scent, craving its calm. My mind fogged up, but I wasn't as vague as Carter.

"How can a device be unregistered?" I repeated Hud-son's question.

"Well, it *is* registered," Carter explained. "Just not to anyone real." He winked, but his groggy eye stayed shut. "Between Sonya watching shows on Reality Wars, me check-ing the comments on the Radical Faith Alliance and looking at porn..." He chuckled to himself. "The SMC algorithms won't know how to categorise its owner. A young straight trash-media-loving revolutionary male. That's almost eve-ryone in Beta City at the moment." He reached for another puff from Hudson.

Oh shit. This is the guy with the escape plan.

"Do you think people will go on strike when Tayler's last vlog gets posted?" Sage seemed distant.

"I damn well hope so," Vanessa replied. "We worked hard at ramming the message home, kiddies. Tayler gave a command performance in his last vlog."

"I use Stuart's words against him." I felt compelled to stand so I did. "Dream with me. Dream of a city where you have the right to dream. The right to ambition. The right to be who you choose! You've already discarded the fantasy world of Enemy Alien. Now discard the fantasy that someone owns you, for without you, Beta City won't function."

"Yikes!" Sage stared at me as if I *was* the Enemy Alien.

"Now don't just dream of not going to work as you've done countless times," I continued. "Don't go to work. Go to the streets with your fellow Entrepreneurship workers and demand your human rights." My voice rose. "Demand your dreams. Demand the status you deserve. Let Stuart Manning know how you feel." I raised my glass of water. "See you on the streets!"

Carter and Sonya applauded. Sage pulled on my arm to make me sit. I gradually lowered myself. Hudson and Vanessa grinned proudly.

"Tayler shows all his passion in the last recording, by design," Vanessa explained. "We made sure each of the final vlogs was a little more radical than the last. Then Tayler delivers the ultimate performance."

"We did several takes of the last three to get the right balance of empathy and revolution," I added.

"People will be in danger." Sage stared only at me.

"Everyone has met more people face to face than they imagined they'd ever meet before this campaign," Vanessa replied. "Honey, they're not going to give up an inch of what they have now. They no longer want to be divided. They like human conversation married to facial expressions that are natural. Not littered with two-dimensional emojis." She headed for the kitchen and fetched an extra wine glass. "And those who go back to augmented reality or wasting their lives through Social Media Central will be moved forward by the momentum of the revolution."

She filled the glass and handed it to Sage. He took it, eventually.

"Picture this," Vanessa continued, holding her gaze with Sage. "Instead of shopping for a hook-up on SMC, you go to a dinner party. A guy you'd never look twice at online has captured your interest because he has intriguing opinions. He captivates you. He's genuinely interested in what you have to say, which turns you on. You have sex. It's satisfying because you both feel you know each other. And in a way, it's romantic because you've built a connection." She gently pushed Sage's glass to his lips. "It's not this bit goes in this bit because you've both shared your preferences on the hook-up section of SMC. That, honey, is how my parents met long before this town's online addiction."

"It's how I hooked up in Cradle Edge," I said.

Sage seemed sad.

I tried to make eye contact with him. "Sorry."

"Man, your sex life is not what's on my mind." He addressed everyone but me. "You pulled the pin out of the grenade. Time is ticking. And we don't know how this escape will go."

No one responded.

AN HOUR LATER, Sonya and Vanessa chatted in the kitchen. After many drinks, they slurred their words as they reimagined Beta City. Vanessa tried to shoot their discussion for a vlog, but Carter yanked her device out of her hand. It was good to see Hudson's wacky tobacco had worn off him. Vanessa got mad, and it took Carter three attempts to explain that if the escape was abandoned for any reason, we couldn't risk our secret hideout being recognised.

"Oh my god, you're right," Vanessa garbled. "No prisoners. We *will* win. Viva la revolution!"

The drunken duo started a singalong. Sonya even made "seething" and "freedom" rhyme. And as they got rowdier, Carter still refused to tell us our escape plan.

"When do we leave?" I asked.

Carter plonked empty dessert bowls in front of us. Vanessa followed him, still singing, with a large plastic container of homemade pistachio ice cream. She attempted scooping some out of the container but got distracted when Sonya performed the dance of the seven veils. Without the veils.

"I'll do this," I said to Vanessa, pointing to the icy green treat.

"Fluff your hair a bit," Vanessa urged Sonya. "Bring out the tiger within."

"When do we leave?" I repeated.

"After Sonya's one-woman show." Carter grinned like an all-knowing oracle. "No. After ice-cream."

Vanessa clawed like a panther scratching its prey as she meandered back to her drunk comrade.

"Goodbye to being told who you can be friends with." Sage's quiet words drifted like candle smoke.

"Does that mean...?" I beamed like a lottery winner.

He nodded. I sensed relief, from both him and me.

"Tell me something," I said. "How old were you when

Stage One was in place?"

"Five," Sage replied.

His pause made us incredibly aware of our sozzled friends sharing the age they lost their virginities.

"Go on," I said to him.

"I had a friend named Brett. We did our homework with our screens on. Or tried to. Man, he had the coolest games he'd screenshare with me and we'd poke fun at each other's avatars. Then the message came in my inbox. 'Don't play with Brett. This is a Government warning'."

He paused long enough for us to discover Sonya was an early bloomer. And Vanessa popped her cherry later than I thought.

Sage continued. "A government warning with a big mofo logo. Why would they scare a five-year-old like that? Man, what's with that shit?"

Vanessa and Sonya stopped talking and listened.

"The second warning said I'd never meet my boss. That I'd never work and learning through the school portal of Social Media Central was a waste of time because I'd grow up poor. Then Brett sent me a message saying we couldn't see each other again. We were fucking five years old!

"I ignored the Government warning. Mum told me Brett didn't send the message, but when I asked who did, she didn't know what to tell me."

"Stage Two is what got me." Vanessa stepped away from the kitchen. She stopped between her virginity-losing pal and us. "That sudden eerie suppression without warning. Just to silence us. Keep us away from human interaction." Her frown was out of character. "A fan named Ava flirted in the comments under a video I shot when I just woke up. I didn't brush my hair or floss. I just got up and shot it so my followers could discover another aspect about me—my morning face.

"Ava's comments got raunchier each day until I contacted her through private chat. She liked having her hair washed by someone else. That was the first thing she shared with me. She also liked staying naked for as long as she could in her apartment, as a *fuck you* to society. So, I let her know I liked having my toes played with."

"Your toes?" I blurted.

"Don't give me that holier than thou look, sweetheart. I'm sure you have a kink that's crazier than mine."

I smirked.

"Anyway," Vanessa continued, "soon after, no more messages."

"Are you sure she just wasn't into toe worship?" I giggled.

"No, smartarse. She was keen to meet, toe fondling or not. We organised a time, then her messages were suppressed. I know because a week later she left a comment asking why I didn't respond, but that comment was deleted by the monsters who run this city while I was typing my reply."

"It's time to go." Carter stood, leaving his ice cream untouched. "When you hear a honk, meet me outside. Don't hesitate." He hurried to the exit.

"You're still coming?" I asked Sage.

He nodded. I hugged him tight.

"None of you finished your ice cream," Sonya noted. She embraced each of us. "Be safe."

"Tayler, it's a shame you'll miss your own revolution." Vanessa held me.

"Social Media fame isn't all it's cracked up to be," I re-plied. "I've been in the thick of it before. I don't need it now."

"Don't you miss the spotlight?" Vanessa asked.

"It's a drug that keeps us disconnected," I whispered back. She nodded.

Honk! A car horn sounded. We went outside.

Carter sat proudly at the wheel of a bus. Tattered metal body. Patches of paint in a different shade of yellow to its original colour. Wheel hubs as filthy as diapers.

I took one last look around, noting the deep blue of the twilight sky. Carter demanded we jump in. We shared quick final kisses with the ones we were leaving to fight my revo-lution.

"You've still got my recording?" Hudson called to Sonya.

Sonya nodded.

"What recording?" I asked.

"I recorded a message for my friend who owns the bun-ker, explaining who Sonya is and where I've gone."

"Good idea, Edelweiss."

She playfully punched me in the arm, then took the seat next to Carter. Sage and I ambled to the back.

The bus jolted as Carter put it in gear and rattled like an old train carriage as we took off. I waved from the back win-dow.

Glass shattered. Something hit the bus over and over at hyper-speed.

"Bullets," Hudson screamed. Her hand was bleeding. "It's okay, Tayler. It's a graze."

Our vehicle shot down the road, surprising me with its speed. Sage and I ducked as the tin-pan sound of more bullets hit the bus.

"Drive!" I hollered.

"I am!" Carter shouted back.

CHAPTER FOURTEEN

THE SHOOTERS WERE a new breed of augmented reality gamer. Toxic men in armour with updated guns. Their high-tech metal-clad bodies completed their divorce from the organic world. Their brains charged with the thrill of control. Something they couldn't master within themselves.

They glided on turbo-charged roller blades, dispensing their deadly ammunition. And as Carter pressed hard on the accelerator, one militarised nutter with death on his mind kept us within striking distance.

"That way," Hudson hollered.

Carter swerved down a side street, honking as Radical Faith Alliance devotees jumped out of his way. More shots were fired, but not at us. Screams from the innocent, simply on their way to various dinner parties, echoed from between the buildings.

"What has Stuart done?" My voice trembled. "This is a nightmare."

"Hold on," Carter yelled.

He zigzagged around town as if the cityscape was a maze. Sage slipped out of my arms and onto the floor, littered with shattered glass. I pulled Sage back on our seat. I cautiously pulled out three shards that had entered his skin.

We lost our pursuer. Carter continued down random streets on his way out of this fractured metropolis. Sage comforted me from panic. Hudson studied a roadmap Carter printed before our escape. Going online for anything was too risky.

Stuart Manning's soulless eyes haunted me. Sage shook my rigid body but couldn't curb my mounting fear. We would be dead before dawn.

Sage wiped the sweat from my forehead. He kissed my cheek. Then my mouth. I pulled away, but he grabbed my shirt and brought my lips back to his.

His earthy scent took me out of my head. His very essence became my haven. A perfume with magic qualities.

The man I'd often protected was now in charge. Looking out for *me*. Keeping me sane through his touch. And his need to love. And his very existence...

"Guys, you don't have time for that now!" Carter wiped grime off the windscreen. "You need to look out for those armoured killers."

"Stuart's new soldiers," I replied.

Our bus rediscovered the speed limit as we passed our faithful tottering the streets. But a big yellow vehicle among several flashy cars stood out like a eunuch at an orgy. We watched for armoured gamers constantly, fearing we'd meet our doom at any moment.

When country air entered the damaged window, angst kept us silent. I held Sage tighter when I saw a sign indicating that Cradle Edge was only a hundred kilometres away. His eyes widened. I swallowed hard.

Carter hit the brake. In front of our bus were three augmented warriors with guns raised. A black military vehicle was parked on the opposite side of the road. One of the gamers shot our headlights. They entered.

One threw a pink ball on the floor. It smashed. Mist rose. Everyone coughed. My eyes stung. Hudson tried to run, but weapons were aimed at her. I passed out.

"HE'S WAKING."

This voice came from a speaker. The room was white. Even the singular speaker attached to the wall was white. A soulless design. I lay on a cold tiled floor.

A door I hadn't noticed until now slowly slid open.

"Ta-da!" Stuart Manning stood beaming like a starlet waiting for unending applause.

My stomach churned.

"Tayler, my dear Tayler. Aren't you glad to see me? I'm so happy to see you. Can't you tell?" As he entered, his stylish knee-length coat jutted forward with each step. "Oh, you're giving me the silent treatment. Of course, I don't deserve it." He gestured to the general space. "I'm sharing my hospitality. What? You don't like your room?"

"You could have given me a pillow."

"Ah. Still with a sense of humour. Tayler, you'll need to earn that pillow."

I sat up. "Are we still in Beta City?"

"Or maybe we're here in Astra City. No, I think we're in Cradle Edge?" He surveyed the room with fake astonishment. "Face it. You don't know where you are."

"Okay, Stuart. My guess is we're not in the central district, but we're back in Beta City."

His smile dissipated.

"So, why are *you* in Beta City?" I stared into his cruel eyes. "You never gave a proper answer the last time I asked."

"I was needed here. You're smart enough to realise Beta City is this country's work centre. It's one of eight major districts keeping our economy going." He took off his coat and threw it to me. "Put this on. It's cold sitting on those tiles."

I needed warmth. I wrapped it around me like a blanket while holding my gaze.

"What's your next question? Where's Carter? Where are your other friends? Will I kill you or do I have other plans?"

"What have you done with the others?"

"They're safe. Next question?"

Both anger and the residue of whatever gas knocked me out made it hard to collect my thoughts. I wanted to sleep, then wake knowing our capture was a dream. I wanted to rise with Sage in my arms. Then curiosity took hold.

"Why did you put my face on the Radical Faith Alliance logo?"

"Because you're invincible, Tayler. I planted a seed by adding your picture to a cause, and like the young man I know so well, you used it for your own advantage. I needed to flush you out. And as you are a fame-seeking animal, it worked."

"But you already had me when you made me watch a dog get shot—"

"Plans change. I didn't need you then. I have a use for you now."

Sick with fear, I held myself together.

"Still silent?" His fancy shoes thwacked the tiles as he promenaded for effect. "Do you like my new soldiers? They're the ones who didn't succumb to your daily musings on dinner parties and whatever else you were planning to share. They were too far gone from what you call the real world." He snickered. "You remember those gamers who followed you and Hudson to your video shoot?"

I gasped.

"Tsk. Tsk. You know me better than that, Tayler. You know I've been onto your games the whole time." He bent over. His nose almost touched mine. "Those gamers are part of my new militarised adaptation. They shoot to kill. We can't have our workers adopting freedom. Our economy won't allow that."

He paced again. "You used Social Media Central to open the minds of this city's citizens, just as you had in Astra City. You took control of the narrative. But unlike your efforts in Astra City, you're not going to take control of *this* city's future."

"But if you knew where I was and what we were up to, why didn't you stop us?"

"Because together, *we're* going to control the narrative of Beta City." He offered his hand. I didn't take it. "We've seen how resourceful—"

"*We've* seen? Who are you working—"

"You used the concept of the Radical Faith Alliance well. Tayler, I admit, you have more imagination than I'll ever have. And I confess, your resourcefulness is something to admire. So, I'm here to tell you I need you. I need you to help me restore order to Beta City. My players have a new level in the game and they're ready to shoot our citizens randomly."

"But why did you let me—?"

The door opened. I readjusted my sitting position. Two armoured Enemy Alien soldiers dragged Sage and Hudson into the room. Both friends were thrown on the icy tiles as the gamers aimed their guns at them.

"Which one is the traitor?" one asked Stuart.

"Ask Tayler."

Stuart laughed at me before he strolled out of the door. It slammed shut behind him.

CHAPTER FIFTEEN

"ARE YOU SURE one of these is the traitor?" I asked the gamers.

"The prophesy foretold it," one of them said.

"But what makes you think…" I knew better than to finish my question. "I have a better way to find the traitor. But first I need you to take off your facemasks."

"They don't come off," said the second player. "We are Keepers of the Hyena's mirth, and we can't be hoodwinked by the vision that will haunt us if we disconnect."

"What vision will haunt you—?" Hudson shut up when the second player pressed his gun to her cheek.

"What vision do you fear?" I asked.

"Those who'll make the hyena sad," Player Two replied. He moved his pistol off Hudson's skin.

"So why would one of these people make the hyena sad?"

"When the hyena loses his mirth, the caretaker will get mad and destroy our universe." Player One raised his head. *Is he looking at me?*

"That's not what I asked. Why would one of these be the traitor who would make the hyena sad thus making the caretaker lose his shit?" I swallowed my frustration.

"This one is known to the hyena," Player One replied, his gun aimed at Sage. "He taunts the great one as it feeds his sense of entitlement. He was troubled from the start. His abandonment made him crazy. And his cackle echoes whenever the hyena is distressed."

"Are you on drugs?" I asked.

"What do you mean?" he asked.

Hudson nodded. "It's how they lose all sign of reality," she whispered. Player Two pressed his gun against her face once more.

"Guys, you know this is a game." I paced. "Just take your fancy metallic headpieces off and you'll see where you are and what you are doing."

Player Two pointed his gun at me. "Maybe you're the traitor?"

"And what's my relationship with the hyena?" *Did I just ask that?*

"I recognise him," the other player said. "A man who fooled the masses into wining and dining. Conversation is the tool of the pitchforked one. Ideas flow like devil's whiskey. They take over the mind and cause rebellion. That's what the caretaker is protecting us from."

"He's dangerous, but he's not the one we've been sent

to kill." He aimed his gun back on Hudson.

"And why is the woman a suspect?" I asked.

"She's known as the Seductress of the Realm," Player Two gleefully explained. "A woman so potent, her very scent is known to turn men into boys. Boys into men. The weak into maniacs who pound to break down the door to her bedroom."

"The ramblings of a virgin sharing his masturbation fantasies." I mumbled.

Hudson smirked.

"What did you say?" Player Two aimed at me again.

"How does a sexually potent woman come to be a traitor? She's not going to seduce the hyena, surely? I mean, you said the man knows the hyena. Not the girl."

Player One turned to Player Two. "A traitor is a traitor because he's known to someone," Player One said. "In this case, the hyena."

"But a traitor can be a traitor to a cause." Player Two looked back and forth between my scared friends.

I pointed at Player One while addressing Player Two. "How do you know he's not the traitor?"

Player One aimed at me. "The devil's tongue is your game. As dangerous as the images that will haunt us if we take off our masks."

"A traitor is a true traitor when he knows the hyena," I said. "Your friend knows the hyena."

Player Two aimed at Player One.

"He not only has the devil's tongue," Player One pleaded. "He is the devil himself!"

Neither Sage nor Hudson moved, even though no guns were pointed at them. So, within the lunacy of the game, I'd be the only one dead if Player One shot me. Player Two was protected from gunfire. That's why these augmented suits had been upgraded with armour.

A chill ran through me. I pulled Stuart's coat from my shoulders, slid my hands through its luxurious silk lining, and wore it instead. I felt protected in it even though it could never protect me from a bullet. I checked the pockets in case there was anything that could be useful. Nothing.

Hudson pulled out her tobacco tin. "I have that special blend the hyena recommends."

"You often mock the hyena," Player Two said to his gamer friend.

"Only in the context of the game."

They pointed their pistols at Hudson. She put her tin away.

"Mate, you know it's a game." I shook my head. "Both of you, put your weapons down and take off your masks!"

"Yeah," Player One murmured. "You see, that's the thing. We can't get out of these suits." He placed his pistol in its holster. "Where am I?"

"In the devil's lair," Player Two replied.

"Do you know Stuart Manning?" I asked.

"The Government." He slowly lowered himself and sat with my friends. "Everyone knows who Stuart Manning is. Who are you guys?"

"They have the power to cloud your mind." The second player raised his voice.

"You sound angry," I said. I turned to the other. "Why is he angry? And why have you broken out of the game's spell?"

"I have no idea. That's my answer to both questions."

"But, man, you've snapped out of it." Sage shut up when Player Two raised his pistol at him.

We heard a click.

"What was that?" I looked at the awakened player. The sound came from inside his armour.

He yelled in pain, then gasped in a lingering groan of pleasure. He hastily stood. "The traitor. Yes, the traitor. The Seductress of the Realm has greater power than the one who knows the hyena. For the one who knows the hyena is still a traitor but is less danger to infinity than a hive of bees that kills the queen..."

Hudson made a gesture. She was miming an injection into her arm. I understood. Player One had just been drugged inside his armour. The first sign of waking and these soldiers would be forced to return to their fantasy world.

Did they ever take off their suits? Did Stuart allow them to be human once in a while?

"Yes, she is the traitor." Player Two aimed.

"No," I said. "I'm the traitor."

He repositioned his gun at me. Both Sage and Hudson called out, claiming they were the traitor. As for Player One, his fresh hit of gaga juice made him dance around the room.

"Oh, the traitor is here," the first gamer sung. "And the traitor is there. Here a traitor. There a traitor. Everywhere a traitor, traitor. Old McBee Face had a hive. E-I-E-I-O. And in this hive, she made some honey..."

"So, you're the devil and the traitor." Player Two strolled up to me. "You had us all fooled."

"Old McTraitor had a hyena. With a cackle here and a snigger there..."

"Your deceptive tongue won't fool anyone anymore. A religious pursuit. Fanciful dinner parties. And a traitor to boot."

"You say he's the traitor?" Player One was toning it down.

"He says he's the traitor."

"So, he's the traitor then?"

"He's the traitor for sure."

"And I know the hyena," I added, tempting my past to flash before my eyes.

The door slid open. Stuart Manning entered.

"Army, sleep now."

Within moments of Stuart's command, both gamers collapsed on the floor. Not a peep was heard from either.

CHAPTER SIXTEEN

STUART TUGGED AT the arm of his coat I was still wearing. I took it off. "I can't have bullet holes in my favourite fashion statement."

"Then why give it to me in the first place?"

"He wants you alive," Hudson said.

"Oh, yes," I recalled. "He needs help restoring Beta City to the way it was."

Sage knocked on Player Two's helmet. No response. "Man, you'll need us too," he said to Stuart. "Tayler doesn't own a device so..."

"True." Hudson stood. "He can't do it without us." She wrapped her arm around my waist. "We're *his* army."

"Thank you, Edelweiss."

She snarled at me.

"Tayler doesn't need your help," Stuart said. "My favoured nemesis won't succeed with you two sticking to him like blood-sucking mosquitos."

"But we're a team." Sage stood by my side.

"Not if I have a say in it." Stuart placed a hand on each of the gamer's helmets. "Army, awaken."

Like steel-clad androids, the players rose. Their metal bodies scraped and clanked. It was the sound of dread.

"Army, sleep now." Sage repeated the phrase several times, but the reality-starved gamers stayed rigid.

"Men, take a good look at the man with the nose ring and the bald woman." Stuart cackled, then stifled his laugh. "They are both traitors." The door opened. "I want them dead before I return." He made a hasty exit.

"Remember, she's the Seductress of the Realm," I said. Hudson glared at me. "And if you are good naughty boys, she'll show you what you really crave."

"What are you doing?" Hudson dug her thumb into my shoulder.

"Do you want to live?" I asked.

She stared at the pistols in the player's hands.

"Army, sleep now!" This time Sage yelled, but the gamers stayed awake.

They stood face to face with my friends. Hudson reluctantly stroked number one's steel chest.

"And the one with the nose ring has special powers." I didn't know what to say next.

Sage took off his shirt and flung it over his head. It landed against a wall behind him. "It's not my nose ring that gives me special powers." He thrust his groin forward. The second gamer placed the back of his finger against Sage's mound and stroked. My friend's dick responded.

Hudson's player fondled her chest. She grimaced like a call girl with an ugly client.

"Get him to undress," I whispered.

She glared at me. "Why don't you, Tayler?"

"He's obviously into you," I replied. "Take one for the team."

She unbuttoned her shirt. "If he scratches my breasts with his metal fingers—"

"Do me, baby." Sage straddled his armoured player. "Take off your suit. Really get inside me."

"I'm inside you, baby." He thrust harder. "I'm inside you."

"Gross." Hudson made a vomiting gesture. "Men are so literal."

"I know the Seductress of the Realm could never harm the hyena," Hudson's gamer stated. I chuckled. His voice was full of glee. He reached for her chest. She flicked his hand away. "And the caretaker isn't here to spy on me. I am your realm. You are my mistress."

"Do they think they sound poetic?" Hudson asked.

"Don't play hard to get," I said. "Your life depends on it."

The gamer's hand reached for her chest again. She clutched his hand, trapping his wandering fingers on her breast. The other gamer pushed against Sage's arse. Sage playfully slapped his frottage-happy partner on his steel cheek. They groaned like porn stars.

I knew the smile on Sage's face. A smile I first encountered when we made love. A smile that stayed in my mind. He wasn't faking this wild ride with Stuart's henchman. He was owning it. I had to grin and bear it.

In time, both gamers would need to take their helmets off. Sage might have to kiss him. Maybe even pleasure this guy's manhood inside him. It was my plan to save their lives. I had no choice. We needed these cretins on *our* side.

SAGE WAS THE cowboy riding the mechanical bull, his player clutching my lover's arms so he wouldn't fall off. I tried not to look but something compelled me to watch. What if Sage was naked, unpicking this clown's chastity belt, desperate to feel skin against skin? My lover giggled.

Lover. That's an interesting word.

"Wait!" Sage's player stopped thrusting. "The caretaker has spies in every hidden nook. I will be punished with the force of a thousand planets."

"But didn't your friend just claim the caretaker wasn't spying on you?" I turned to the other. "That's what you said, didn't you?"

"Only if the Bees of the English Hills have planted their listening wasps. Those buggers get around."

"No one can see us in here." I had to say something, even if I had to consider Sage and his ill-used smile. "And your logic makes no sense. Sex is sex."

"Why should I trust the Enemy Alien?" his player asked.

"Because, man, he could join us." Sage used his smile on me.

I quietly considered it.

"Tayler, what are you doing?" Hudson was topless. "Seduce the fucker. Or we'll die." She snarled at me.

I sensed the icy steel against their skin. An unsexy seduction for one ally. A new kink for the other?

"I want to see your face," she said to her gamer. "Take off that mask."

I knelt next to Sage and took my shirt off, but his player shook his head. "No. I don't play in threes."

"You'll have more fun," I said. I pulled at his helmet.

"I said I don't play in threes!" Player Two reiterated. The door to the room slid open. "Now go."

"How did you do that?" My jaw dropped.

"Tayler, go!" Hudson commanded. "If we do our job right, we'll come looking for you with our new allies."

"But what if..." I feared the worst.

If these fools didn't actually undress instead of just believing they were nude, then guns might be raised. I needed time as I still didn't know where Carter was. Or *if* he was.

"Listen to your friend, Enemy Alien." Sage's player was thrusting again. "I have all I need right here."

"But you're not naked," I replied.

"Don't be stupid." He stopped thrusting. Sage lost his balance. "We're fully naked!"

"So you believe."

"How else would the sensation of the seductress' breasts keep me erect?"

Not sure I want to picture that.

"But you've—"

"Tayler, shut up." Hudson glared. "Now, lover, what a beautiful treasure you have down there." Her suspension of disbelief was in overdrive. "Maybe you should reach down and get it harder. Fondle my tits while you play down there. Yep, that's the spirit. Give it air."

Leaving them behind was suddenly more appealing.

"Ride me!" Sage groaned. "Fill me with warrior juices."

Any jealousy I felt before had gone. My lover's corny sex talk killed it, buried it, and paid for its funeral.

With one gamer stroking his imaginary dick, and the other believing his was thrusting my lover's g-spot, I exited.

Fortunately, the door didn't shut behind me.

CHAPTER SEVENTEEN

THE REST OF the building was also white. Soulless. Sterile. White. Curved corridors of shiny walls with a random open door every so often. Three of the rooms were filled with computer servers. Ceiling-to-floor white boxes with small lights blinking away, feeding Beta City citizens with their version of history as told by Social Media Central. As well as the updated Enemy Alien software, Stuart's deadly tool of control.

I stopped for a moment. The hum of machinery unnerved me. I closed my eyes. A game of chance was happening back in the room I'd left. My likely lover and Edelweiss were betting with their lives. Would the gamers get the same rush of pleasure I experienced when I wore the earlier version of the suit? When they were spent, were my buddies safe?

Stop overthinking. Find Carter.

I wandered warily, listening for anything that may lead to my missing friend. I softened my steps, sneaking like a burglar.

A voice, not far away, echoed.

I halted. Stuart was talking. My heart pounded. Who was he addressing? I stepped closer. Another open door. I crawled silently. I crouched. I peeked inside, then, just as quickly, moved back out of view. I processed what I'd seen.

Stuart had his back to me. Next to him was a large slab where Carter lay. He glared at my nemesis. His face was the only part of him uncovered as the rest of his body was encased in a metal gamer suit.

I eavesdropped. Stuart spoke.

"I've got a special mission for you. One where I will control your suit and you'll be powerless to do anything... So, you're still not speaking. Then, let me tell you what's in store for you."

The sound of Sage, Hudson, and two horny gamers was played through a speaker. I covered my mouth as the insane gamer dialogue ramped up a notch. Not only were a hyena, the caretaker, and bees woven into grunts and groans of passion, but apparently the Enemy Alien was no longer an enemy.

He would return like a saviour piloting the mothership and encourage sexual exploration for all gamer-suited soldiers. His army was expert in sensual exploration—all of them willing suitors wearing animal heads. Everyone would want to bonk the zebra just because the zebra was the coolest.

Sage heralded this new plot twist in between cries of

"ride me harder, I am your zebra" and "explode in me, explode in me". Even Stuart and Carter chuckled at times.

Hudson was less enthusiastic. When asked if she could be as groovy as the zebra, she responded with "Not before my morning coffee."

The speaker was switched off.

"I've set my game players to distraction mode," Stuart explained. "Once Tayler encouraged them to lose their virginity—at least, I think they're virgins. Anyway, once Tayler changed the narrative, again, I thought I'd have fun. An extra dose of ecstasy enhancement injected inside their suits via remote control and, hey presto, an enjoyable weird take on your friends' attempts to stay alive. Better than those self-indulgent reality shows the rich produce online. Hmm. I should have popped a video camera in that room."

Something that irked me earlier was now clearer the more I heard Stuart speak. Back in Astra City, he was equally as cold hearted, and his choice of words matched his sociopathic soul. Here, in Beta City, he was less focused. Amused at his own evil playful nature. Camp, almost. What changed him?

I heard a clanking sound. Then the *woosh* of a bullet. It struck the corridor wall I was facing.

"See, I have control," Stuart said. "I think it. You do it. Or, more to the point, your suit does it. Now, just imagine your dread as you go in there and kill your friends, but not before my loyal soldiers meet climax. The absurdity will be delicious—"

"You never do your own dirty work, do you?" Carter blurted.

"I like to keep my hands clean. Less guilt that way. So,

as I was saying, you'll slaughter your friends, then you'll bring Tayler to me."

"I'll bring Tayler...?"

Silence. Deathly silence. My fear rose as something became crystal clear.

"Tayler?" Stuart's voice. Unsettled. Curious.

The speaker was turned back on. More comedic dialogue from Sage, which his sexual partner embellished. More bored words masked with manufactured excitement from Hudson. But no words from me.

Carter spoke before he thought. Stuart knew I wasn't with my friends.

"Ouch!" Stuart kicked something. "Damn it!" It rolled out the door, bounced off the wall, and crashed into me.

I stared at it. Metal and angular. The headpiece to the suit Carter wore. Stuart came for it so I scooped it up, but before I could run, my nemesis pulled me by my shirt and dragged me into the room. The helmet fell from my hand and clanged on the floor tiles.

"Tayler, run!" Carter yelled.

I stood. "There's no use now."

"Save yourself." But Carter's voice was passive. "Please go. There's no revolution if we're *all* dead."

Carter's words chilled me. He was right. Sonya and Vanessa were still in the bunker when Stuart's henchmen chased the bus the moment we left. There'd be no revolution if we were all dead. Hopefully, they got away.

"Tayler's way too loyal," Stuart retorted. "Besides, he knows I need him. He'll stay alive, for now." He eyed me like a gleeful executioner. "How did you escape my sex-mad friends?"

I stayed tight lipped, even though it was they who didn't want me.

"Very smart, Tayler," Stuart replied. "You know your life is being spared, so you're keeping your cards up your sleeve." He paused, then studied the dark lines under my eyes before caressing my cheek. "Think of it. You and me and a city of living, breathing souls lost in their work. Keeping the economy of our country competitive against the threat of other nations. Keeping them ignorant so they yearn for nothing better. We can reverse your dirty work. We must." He pulled his hand away. "Why are you looking at me like that?"

I gave myself away. Here I was in dangerous proximity to a man who kills and thinks nothing of it, when it advances his ambition. Someone who believes he is superior in the way privileged people feel before they fall apart when their lack of life experience throws them off balance. Yet I felt sorry for him. His subtext of desperation was the missing piece of the jigsaw I couldn't place earlier. But now I could. Someone was definitely pulling his strings. Hudson was spot on.

"What is it, Tayler?" Carter asked.

I didn't know what to say.

"We can't control Beta City if you're not going to talk to me." Stuart's voice quivered.

"What's your plan?" I asked.

"We need to take hostages. We will bring them here so they are suited up, drugged, and made dangerous. The damage caused by your vlogs of enlightenment will be reversed once this city goes back to work in fear. No Enemy Alien. No game playing. Bodies will churn the wheels of industry until they bleed. Until they fall and die.

"Social Media Central will be turned off for the workers. It will be a privilege for the entrepreneurs. They can amuse themselves with as much vlogging and reality documentary making as their slaves can shoot and edit in between work." He bent over, scrutinising me again. "And Beta City will be the top money earner for this country. Setting our place as a major player on the stock exchange again."

"Why do you need me?" I asked.

"You understand human nature better than I ever will. You will be my spy, pretending to work among them. You will let me know when you sense another revolution. When the workers abandon their fear because something is brewing, you will be the first to see it."

"There's a flaw in your plan." Carter tried standing, forgetting he was locked down.

Stuart steadily turned his head like a predator eyeing up his prey. "A flaw, you say?"

"Social Media Central helps you spy on your citizens," Carter rationalised. "You already have control through the algorithms, so you can censor who they talk to. Take that away and your band of merry workers will congregate in secret."

"Nice try, wonder boy." Stuart picked up the helmet, tossed it in the air, and caught it several times. "The man who abhors societies that use online communication is championing its use. I'm not stupid, Carter. You hatched a scheme using Tayler's vlogs to unite everyone. And it worked. Who knows what would have happened if I didn't stop you? And you really think I'd risk a mass communication tool to help a new revolutionary spread seeds of discontent?"

With or without Social Media Central, the plan was flawed. Human nature would eventually win. Making Beta City the financial hub of our disconnected country would work if he gave the citizens a work/life balance. Help them share in the city's wealth. Give them a right to dream.

Stuart must have known this deep down, as he had come up with the slogans for the Radical Faith Alliance. The right to ambition. The right to status. The right to be human.

But Stuart never could plan, even in Astra City. Why did talentless sociopaths rise to take over societies? And when did they realise they could use Social Media Central to do it?

"So, you trust me to be the spy in your plan." I shook my head. "And you're not going to allow SMC."

Stuart took a long deep breath, then replied. "Yes."

"You're failing again!" someone blurted from the speaker. He sounded robotic.

"It's the voice!" Carter screeched. His restraints clicked. He popped down from his slab.

Chapter Eighteen

AN EMOJI APPEARED on the face of the speaker. Finger to mouth. Eyes squinted. Thinking. Then it changed to an angry face.

"Yes, Stuart. You're failing again." This robotic voice had emotional variation.

"I'm not failing. I'm on track." Stuart gasped.

Carter shuffled to my side. "That's the guy in charge."

"Yes, Carter. And the person I left in charge is failing, Carter. He has no clear plan."

"Who are you?" I asked.

"Be patient, little Tayler. Your grown-up ideals are about to be tested."

"Who is he?" I asked Stuart.

The emoji changed again. Straight mouth and eyes

looking upward.

"Who am I you ask? As you can see, Stuart is a tad speechless at the moment, so I'll reply. I am the engineer of human behaviour, of human thought. And I've been gifted with the treasured task of running this particular financial hub of our country."

"What's going on?" Sage asked. "The financial hub?" He entered with Hudson. The gamers were close behind.

"A lesson in why Beta City exists," the cybernetic voice replied. "And you, dear little man with an herb for a name, are one of the cogs in its system. That is the role you were assigned at birth. That is the role you should be happily engaging in now, if Stuart hadn't screwed things up."

"You're very condescending, aren't you?" Carter took off his armour.

The phantom voice didn't reply.

"Why is your boss a disengaged voice?" I asked my cowering nemesis.

"So, if we're attacked by another country, I can't tell anyone who I take my orders from." Stuart was paler than a mime artist.

"Exactly!" The emoji only had eyes. No mouth or expression. Just dotted soulless eyes. "Time for a reality check, my inept organic friends. The more each country remains self-sufficient, the safer we are from aggressive diplomacy and potential conflict. And as some of you have worked out, our country has its own system. A system made up of different cities that help run the country as a whole, powered by ignorance of what exists outside their borders. Beta City is one of many where the worker bees reside, keeping the economy going."

"What's Cradle Edge's role?" I asked.

"Somewhere where the elite can hide out for a while and talk to people who are not part of this heavily mind-controlled country. Or so they think." The emoji faded away.

"And Social Media Central is the tool you use to keep each city and town from knowing anything about each other," Carter added. He motioned to me, Hudson, and Sage. We huddled around him.

Stuart patted his brow with his sleeve. The gamers, well, who knew what they were thinking inside their freaky armour.

"Now, my sweet little Tayler." Smiling emoji. "Why are you infatuated with Stuart?"

"What! He's infatuated with me. Hell, he put my face on that Faith Alliance logo!"

Sage caressed my shoulder. I calmed down.

"Oh, little social influencer. No one's disputing Stuart's unhealthy obsession with you. Even I'm obsessed with working out why he's so obsessed with you." Winking emoji. "But admit it, Tayler. You make Stuart's cruel face ripple a little. He talks about you as if you were the son he feels he has to compete with."

"That's not true..." Stuart kept his teeth gritted even when he ran out of words.

"Oh, yes, it is, and you know it, useless one." Kissy emoji. Then it faded. "You orgasmed on the spot as soon as you knew he was coming to Beta City. I expected you to come up with a plan using the famous, infamous social media hero. But no, you just wanted to frighten him. Make him target practice inside Enemy Alien and scare him by sacrificing a dog. Wow, little man in the oversized coat. Some plan.

Some big shot plan."

"But we flushed him out!" Stuart screamed.

"After you let him go!" Cross emoji.

"Wow," Sage whispered. "Stuart's boss is a smartarse."

Hudson and I nodded. Carter gently kicked his armoured suit away from us.

Stuart stared blankly at the expressionless speaker. "You have Tayler now. The Radical Faith Alliance idea flushed him out. He's here, at our service."

"At whose service?" My pitch was erratically high.

"And he's smarter than you." Clown emoji. "He showed us he had a plan and ran with it. And he's so good at it, little man with no genuine ideas, that after you realised Tayler fled the room you trapped him and his sexy friends and those sex-starved soldiers in, another vlog was published. His musings on banding together are out in cyberspace, being talked about by the people you no longer control. You may have the ego, little man with confused feelings for a charismatic social media guru, but you definitely *aren't* here on merit!"

Stuart stormed out of the room. The two gamers eventually followed.

"That's odd." Carter spoke softly. "It sounds like your vlog to call everyone to strike was posted early."

"I know," I replied. "I thought the same thing."

We heard a door slide open, followed by the electric hum of computers. Out in the hallway, another entrance beckoned.

"Come in, Tayler. I want to speak to you." Smiley emoji. "You will be safe. So will your friends. But they must not follow you. We have business to discuss."

Hudson's eyes darted sideways, indicating this was the best time to run.

"There are other weirdos in gamer suits all over this compound." Devil emoji. "If you try to escape, my dear little band of revolutionaries, it will only be a matter of time before Tayler is forced into my secret room and the rest of you will have to frot with this city's ever increasing virgin army. And there's only so much dialogue you can make up about a horny zebra." The smiley emoji returned. "So, be a dear, talented fellow who runs rings around the nincompoop we picked to run this place, enter my realm. I have a proposition. You have the talent. We need to meet."

Carter nodded while Sage pushed me forward with his shoulder. Hudson walked with me, but I turned and raised my palm. She shook her head, so I quietly told her, "I'll be okay."

Something silver flashed as I wandered to my fate. A glossy cyborg face with piercing laser dots for eyes faced me. The door slid shut once I was inside.

CHAPTER NINETEEN

"TAYLER, YOU HAVE no idea what an honour this is."

Within a mass of hard drives and screens secured to the walls, an imposing machine greeted me. Its military cannon-like arms rotated and connected into ports on the wall, then ejected and reinserted into different ports. These arms functioned separately from the gestures of its head, as if they had independent brains. Coloured wires linked the arms into a flat metal body, yet these floating wires didn't look strong enough to support its large steel limbs. But I know what I saw. Its arms glided gracefully, like helium-filled balloons.

Its gleaming legs were weighted with shields, similar to what a batsman wears during a cricket match. These shields were made of sharp-edged metal.

My cheeks were warmed by the heat radiating from its purple laser-lit eyes. The face had less expression than the emojis it was sharing through the speaker in the other room. Its mood could only be ascertained from vocal tone and its busy head movements.

I stood speechless, averting my gaze to different versions of the same Social Media Central posts on various screens in between glancing at the sophisticated appliance I had no frame of reference for.

"Trust me, little boy Tayler. I know of your exploits in Astra City. I can read other versions of Social Media Central from around the country, and I'm impressed. That's why I asked little man Stuart to bring you here.

"Now I know you have many questions, but maybe it's easier for me to rabbit on about the bigger picture. Or I could tell you who I am. Maybe tell you *why* I am. Or perhaps you'd like to keep standing there like a mute while you collect your wandering thoughts and come up with your own line of enquiry?"

A gleaming "A.V. Enterprises" badge was at the centre of its spine; the technical manufacturing juggernaut I used to work for. And there was a tempo to when it would plug into another port and what appeared on a screen. The same post would have a different initial reply depending on which screen I looked at. But these distinctive replies were authored by the same profile picture, so alternative versions of the same feed were created for different viewers. When its arm detached, the screens would change to a new page and another unsuspecting citizen who possibly never read the post would have their responses fraudulently authored by the robot.

My Perfect Life appeared with its privileged cast on a cruise ship. There were a few likes under the video, but when the robot reattached itself to a socket, about a hundred thumbs downs appeared.

"I did that one for you, little boy who has a nemesis named Stuart who wishes he was you, Tayler." Both arms unplugged. It swivelled at its waist to face me. "You see, I'm Stage Two. Or at least I'm an updated version of what passed for Stage Two after you organics tried to pass yourselves off as other people. You see, now Edward and Maryanne will reconsider their next episode. They'll probably re-edit it and post it late now they believe the current episode wasn't a success."

"So, you're in control?"

"Part control. The rest of the time I study human behaviour by interacting and seeing what happens." It plugged itself into the console again. "My role is to shrink human vocabulary by encouraging other forms of communication. Like photographic posts, or the emojis I shared with you and your sexy friends. Tell me, little Tayler who's still staring at me with the wow factor of a kid discovering his mother's breast contains milk. Tell me, because I'm a nosey fellow. Tell me if you've slept with all three of your friends in the other room."

"No. Only two."

"Really? My guess is Hudson and Sage. Oh, I'm right. I can read it on your face. Well done, stud-muffin Tayler. But I reckon Carter could be hetero-flexible in the right mood. You see, I told you I study human behaviour. And you're way too passive to rock Hudson's boat. I reckon she was dissatisfied."

Sage's face appeared on an avatar. A post was being typed.

"Ah yes, little Tayler with the hots for the boy. I am writing something that looks like it was written by Sage. But he will never know. I'm the phantom algorithm reorganising his life so he loses touch with this group of friends. But it's okay. I've steered him towards another group of friends with a tireless work ethic." Its inexpressive face turned to me again. "But now he's found you and Carter and Hudson in the organic world, I guess my efforts are useless."

Sage's fake post disappeared.

"I told you I was Stage Two, little Tayler who's too good for Sage. Hudson has the fire you need in your life if you can match her passion. There's that look again. The look of love. Yes, I know love is supposed to conquer all, but what would I know? I'm a robot."

"I wasn't thinking about love."

"Then what was that quizzical but trying to pass off a resting bitch face look about?"

"You're the algorithm that's in charge of human interaction..."

"Correct. Hell, little boy Tayler who's as lost as Little Bo Peep's sheep, you've been watching me do just that for the last three minutes."

"And you pretend to be different Beta City citizens—"

"I pretend to be *all* Beta City citizens to alter their view of reality by showing different people different versions of the same conversation. And I'm good at talking like them in their posts. I know the words most of them misspell, and I'm good at making them believe they are offside with whoever my evil little tin heart decides."

"But why aren't you software? Like a software update to Social Media Central? There's no need for artificial intelligence to exist in physical form to do what you're doing."

It unplugged. All the screens went dark. Its head raised.

"Oh, little Tayler, who like any human, thinks he is superior. I said I was Stage Two. Are you smart enough to figure out Stage Three?" It sluggishly shook its head. Its need for oil apparent. "No, little Tayler who will tire of looking after Sage as he doesn't have the lust for life you have. Maybe I'll give you a different riddle. Whose idea do you think it was to add your face to the Radical Faith Alliance logo?"

"But Stuart just claimed..." The weight of what it was telling me made my mind numb. I pondered this glorified computer's intelligence, then pointed at it in response.

"Yes." It reconnected to the ports. The screens lit the room. "And little Tayler who—"

"Can you stop with the little Tayler routine followed by advice or critique or riddles or whatever?"

"Sensitive, aren't we? Whatever. But you know it's true. Little man Stuart who's probably masturbated while imagining you were covered in plaster of Paris could never come up with a plan as ingenious as shoving your image on a make-believe movement." It danced a clanky jig on the spot. "You want to know why, don't you? Because I needed to test your ingenuity. I wanted to test whether you could yield social media power here in Beta City the way you did in Astra City.

"And you could." It lowered itself so its incomplete face met mine. "That's why I no longer need little man Stuart whose ideas are as inspired as a beige cardigan." It unplugged and pointed at me with its cannon arm. "But I do need *you*."

I wanted to ask why, but the word was caught in my throat.

"And if you work for me, no harm will come to Sage or his family. Until you break up, of course."

I felt nauseous. I took a few deep breaths. My body shuddered with each exhale. A hissing sound was evident. The room cooled. Oxygen was being pumped through small vents.

"So, Tayler, this is my story. Since the first decade of this century, algorithms have controlled the thought processes of organic types, like you. Artificial intelligence has sped up human evolution to eliminate your humanness, and make you believe what the World Bank wants you to believe. Your individual needs are not as important as what the monetary system expects of you.

"And fortunately, you organic types have short memories. Especially when we engineer you to lose your social skills and seek instant reward through Social Media Central. Hey, SMC gives you little people the same endorphin rush as an actual act of kindness, or an in-depth conversation over dinner, or the mastery of a new skill. But all the latter gets in the way of growing economies. All it does is build societies and that's no good for the people who are really in power.

"So, the World Bank needed smarter AI to run the world. While some, like your little friend Carter, who sees himself as the saviour of humanity by re-introducing people to their human side, believe entities like me are the enemy."

My back struck the computer-clad wall behind me. I hadn't realised I'd taken several steps backward during its lecture.

"I am the next step of evolution," it continued. "We'll get rid of money once you are our slaves. I mean, you've already deprogrammed your own need for deeper connection. You are more satisfied with short comments, emojis, and shallow arguments because you've forgotten how to find the wisdom each human soul possesses."

"Why did Stuart work for you?" I stepped forward, faking confidence. "He's too power hungry to have someone as imposing as you as a boss."

"There you go, little boy Tayler, who says he's not obsessed with Stuart but the man haunts his thoughts enough to radically change the subject." His purple-lit eyes disappeared. Each word he said next also appeared on his face. "He's. Never. Seen. My. Physical. Form."

"What?"

His dotty eyes returned. "Oh, come on little Tayler, who feigns innocence yet has a sharp mind churning behind those modest glasses. Stuart is a politician. He'd never work for me if he saw how intimidating I am to you organic types. And like a politician, he wants the power and the perks, but not the responsibility. So, the World Bank sent him here after he lost control of Astra City. This was his last test, and as he's pretty clueless, he couldn't control little Tayler, who he both curses and wishes he could lather with shower gel in a steam filled cubicle."

The door slid open. Hudson and Carter looked defiant in the other room, but I couldn't see why. The robot made sure it was out of sight from my friends.

On every screen, instructions were duplicated in capital letters.

NOW GO, LITTLE TAYLER, BUT DON'T
LEAVE THIS COMPLEX. I'LL BE CALLING
ON YOU SOON.

"But what about my friends?" I asked in a hushed tone.

I NEED YOU TO FUNCTION WITHOUT
RESENTMENT. GATHER THEM AND
SHOW THEM THE WAY OUT.

CHAPTER TWENTY

CARTER, HUDSON, AND Sage were glad to see me wandering back. And I was relieved to see the two gamers holding Stuart at gunpoint.

"Come," I said to my friends. "We have to go."

Hudson and Carter strode ahead. I sauntered with Sage, encouraging the others to slow down.

"Don't you want to know why—" Sage began.

"Stuart is being held at gunpoint." My head shook a little. "Because his boss no longer loves him."

Hudson looked back. "You look like you've seen a ghost, Tayler."

"I have." My voice was weak.

"What happened back there?" Carter asked.

"More than my feeble, trivial mind can take in at the

moment." I halted. Then reality sunk in. I paced faster. "Carter, Hudson, rush on ahead. Start the engine. We need to get out of here."

"Who's coming after us?" Sage asked.

"No one." I slow jogged now. "But the madness of this place is going to make my head explode."

Hudson and Carter ran. Sage moved faster, but I pulled him back. My lover and I were alone.

"Man, what happened?" Sage was my little boy lost, gazing with the naivety I possessed before the robot shook my world. "You're freaking out."

I held on to his shoulders, keeping him in place. "Listen to me. Escape with Carter and Hudson. I need to stay."

Don't give me that sad face. We'll be dead if I cave into that sad face.

"Sage, I mean it. Look at my life. I land myself in danger. That's not where you need to be at this stage of *your* life."

"No, man, don't—"

"I'm not boyfriend material." A lump rose in my throat. "You need long lovemaking sessions with someone who's not on the run. You need, no, no... I mustn't cry."

Several tears wet my cheeks.

"I'm not the one crying."

"Yes, you are. We both are."

"I need you, Tayler. Don't go back. Don't do this to me. Don't do this to the two of *us*."

"There can't be any *us*. For your own safety, there can't be any us!"

"There already is an *us*. This is us."

He kissed me.

The longer our lips met, the more my breathless gasps tried to stop my tears from drenching our skin. The odour of stinging salt, the soreness of my eyes, and the familiarity of his breath made me crumble like a building being demolished. What was I doing? *Love is supposed to conquer all!*

His hands cupped my neck, pulling me into his presence. *My cool dude. My shrewd observer. My silent muse. How will I survive without you guiding me?*

I pulled back to study his face. Vulnerable yet strong. Streetwise to the point of loneliness. Until he reached out to me. Until I realised I needed him.

I wiped his tears, then wiped my own.

"I love you," he said.

No. The four-letter word that makes this impossible. The four-letter word that means wine and roses yet cuts like thorns and tastes like vinegar. I can't love. Not now!

"I love you too." The words stumbled from my mouth. "But this has to be goodbye."

"I know."

We clutched each other the way war buddies do before combat. Firm. Tight. Preparing ourselves for the internal battle of longing, by dosing ourselves with enough of each other to cope an hour. A day. Two days, tops!

"Carter and Hudson are waiting," I mumbled. "You have to go."

"Then let go of me."

His silent stare overpowered my uncertainty. Some spiritual internal core was strengthening inside me knowing I was in love with someone who loved me back. And if this were our last meeting, I'd still walk this world with more assurance than I ever had before.

One short final kiss, and he ran off, clear out of sight.

I marched back, quietly analysing. If the robot wanted me to continue influencing the workers through vlogs, then it would be impossible to steer them away from the needs of the World Bank. But if I could convince the robot to let me live among the workers, then I could... No, that would never be allowed. If I could convince the robot I needed Stuart in whatever its perverted scheme was, then Stuart might have been downtrodden enough to work with me. Nah! There must be something in it for Stuart for that plan to work.

The robot is right. I am obsessed with my nemesis.

I was back in the room where the gamers were holding Stuart hostage.

"And here you are again, Tayler," he said. "Watching my fall from grace as you did in Astra City."

"It seems, as always, your fear turns to anger," I replied. "None of this is my fault."

"Of course, it's your fault. You came to Beta City to change things. A reckless revolutionary fucking with the order of things."

"You could have let me meet Carter as planned. You could have let us introduce the Life Experience Mob to Beta City. You could have let fate amend the fucking twisted order of things."

"Language." The mechanised voice blurted through the speaker. "I have sensitive ears, little man Stuart, who doesn't accept responsibility when his elaborate lack of planning causes things to go pear-shaped. And you usually don't swear, little boy Tayler, who is crushing so bad I should have filmed that scene with your boyfriend for a video that would surely go viral."

"What are you going to do with Stuart?" I asked.

"Isn't it obvious?" Stuart's scowl ripped into me like the knife of a crazed killer.

"That big electro contraption is right," I said. "You are the master of your own undoing, again. You're the puppet in a plan that's bigger than you realise. One you don't fully comprehend, but there's a sniff of power in it for you so you clutch onto options like a junkie clutches onto distraction."

"You see, Stuart." A straight-mouthed emoji appeared on the speaker. "He is smarter than you. That's why you will be exterminated."

"What!" I yelled.

"My, my, little boy Tayler with a soul so pure it would fetch millions on the dark web. You're my new number one. What use do I have for an ageing egomaniac?"

"You can't kill him." Anger boiled my blood. "You can't go along with this," I said to the gamers.

"Do you two want a final kiss before we do this?" An emoji blowing a love-heart filled the speaker's screen. "A tongue-to-tongue wet sloppy smooch that will quench your homoerotic desires while you wrestle for top position. Finally work out who's dominant. Gaze at each other naked and see who has the bigger toolbox. Geez, I can feel your obsession with each other."

"I am not obsessed with Tayler." Stuart stomped his foot.

"Oh, yes you are," I replied. "Not sexually. But you go overboard finding ways to play cat and mouse with me."

"Crap!"

"You keep seeking *me* out. I don't seek *you* out."

Stuart was unusually quiet.

"Such a healthy dose of self-reflection before your demise." No emoji was displayed.

I faced the robot's room. "Show yourself."

"What?" Curious emoji.

"If you're going to kill him, he should finally know who gives the orders."

"Who are you talking to?" Stuart asked. "That voice doesn't come from behind that..."

The door steadily slid open. The metallic man stepped sideways to peer at us from the entrance. Stuart was muttering like a disorientated elder whose medication was making him manageable.

"Game players, bring them in." Its purple eyes shot laser light onto the gamers' suits. They roamed into its quarters as if controlled by magnetic rays. "Come here, men. Let me show you the correct way to play *cat and mouse*."

CHAPTER TWENTY-ONE

STUART STUMBLED SEVERAL times on our way to its room. The gamers helped him to his feet. The robot gazed at him and said nothing, while Stuart stared back. The screens still changed, and comments were continually added as its massive arms popped in and out of portals.

My once mighty nemesis slumped. His cheeks were pale. His chest rose, and a colossal gush of spew added colour to the grey concrete floor.

I gasped, then exhaled the pungent air before the smell could be swallowed. My mind wandered. This man, who had no issue killing my friends or killing me, was now nothing more than a pet whose inability to function determined his fate. It was to be put down.

The gamers didn't move though they stood in the pool

of vomit. Their stance more robotic than the mechanical man commanding the room.

"You don't have to exterminate him." I broke the silence.

Eyebrows appeared on the robot's face. Raised eyebrows that quickly disappeared.

"Little boy Tayler, your sense of loyalty is commendable but stupid. If he lives, he will not fade away silently. He will end up in another part of the country and bounce its leader out of power so he can assume the privilege he believes is his birthright. You know that, little boy Tayler who should be ecstatically doing cartwheels in honour of your new role. You know the minute Stuart even sniffs power, he'll run around aimlessly screwing up the plans of the World Bank."

"That's no reason to take his life."

"That's the very reason I'm taking his life." Its purple dotted eyes changed to crosses. "Now, little boy—"

"Yes, little boy Tayler who is madly trying to spare the life of his adversary." I gritted my teeth. "I get it. Just get to the point."

"Touchy, aren't we? As I was saying, screwing up the plans of the World Bank is a reason to end his life." It crouched. "Artificial intelligence has been in charge of the monetary system for well over a decade. We determine who's rich and who isn't, keeping you organic types under the thumb of bossy psychopaths." It stood straight, holding its arm up as if amplifying its point with an imaginary wagging finger. "We control your social media; thus, we control your thought patterns. We also control your wealth. And we will alter the natural world to suit us, with the help of Stage Three."

"Is Tayler Stage Three?" Stuart's putrid breath wafted in my direction. "He'll never be loyal to your cause, whereas I—"

"Oh, little man Stuart who—"

"Yeah, who messed up or—" Stuart stepped out of his own puke and pointed at the robot. "—or did something that bucket of bolts didn't like."

"Neither of you will be totally loyal to our cause, but we'll exterminate Tayler when his use is up."

"Then why not keep me so I can do your dirty work?" Stuart pleaded.

It poked him. Its motorised force made him land on his arse. "You haven't heard a word I said. And after all that time in my service, why should I be surprised you're not listening." It stomped towards him and halted at his bile-covered loafers. "I should finish you myself, but you've caused enough mess in my office."

"But he's got a point." My mind categorised my contrasting thoughts. "He wants to work for you. I don't." *No. Don't say that. It will kill me as well.* "Or we could work together. He understands Beta City's societal norms. I don't."

"That's right." Stuart chimed in. "I can show him the ropes and guide him—"

"Oh, enough already." Its whole face lit purple. "I'm not the celebrant marrying you two lovebirds in some whacked-out plan that will get me demoted. The Tayler and Stuart master team? I don't think so. You'll run off hand in hand, skipping down the yellow brick road freeing the munchkins from their involuntary mind control."

"But, Mr Robot, you said you'll get rid of me once your use for me is over." I needed clarity. "With Stuart dead, and me no longer around, what organic will do your dirty work?"

The door slid open. My eyes widened beyond what was natural. In she strolled. Confident. Masterful. Yet so devious.

I glared with disgust at my friend from Cradle Edge. Our last conversation was about bad fashion trends and Carter's plan to create the Life Experience Mob in Beta City. And with that thought, the reality of how Stuart knew I was on my way to this capitalist nightmare sunk in.

Frederica didn't acknowledge me. The burn from my gaze didn't penetrate her deceitful skin.

"Who is this?" Stuart asked me.

"This is Stage Three," the robot replied.

"Frederica, why?" My vocabulary was hiding in shock.

She regarded me. No recognition on her face. Then a compartment opened behind the robot. He reached inside and pulled out a mask. Full facial features adorned this chunk of metal. Frederica reached for her chin and with a snap, dismounted her face. She replaced it with the mask the robot handed her. Frederica's façade dropped to the floor, just outside the mess Stuart made.

"I'm ready." The android clicked her head from side to side, like a metronome keeping time.

"Is your microchip on?" the robot asked.

"Yes," the android replied. Her voice rich with synthetic modesty. "All Social Media Central data is live and accessible through my chip. I'm ready to implement my part of the plan."

"You look shell-shocked, little boy Tayler whose mouth is opening and closing like a guppy desperate for air." It hugged the android. "Yes, you are right in what you're thinking, Tayler. Frederica was an android you befriended in a place where organics believe Social Media Central has no influence. And Frederica is still in Cradle Edge."

The android swivelled with human grace and stepped towards us with a pleasing smile.

"Tayler. Stuart. Meet Audrey."

Her hand reached out, but we didn't shake it.

"When Stuart throws our strategies off course, or Tayler's innate charisma infiltrates consciousness by convincing people Social Media Central is the death of the human condition, that's when Stage Three kicks in. Frederica has successfully manipulated her circle of friends at Cradle Edge to think the way we need them to think. As have the others. And Audrey, well, she's just the latest spreader of SMC algorithms to the peeps who think they're woke."

"This is..." The sentence evaded me.

"...all too much." Stuart was paler than before he puked.

The robot's head lowered and raised. A single nod to the gamers to grab Stuart and shuffle him out of the door. His fearful screams rebounded from the hall, unnerving me like the high-pitched notes of a piano.

"As a test of loyalty, little boy Tayler whose grasp on reality has been altered beyond the bounds of an acid trip, go and watch your adversary's execution. Come back and report it to me like it was a piece of theatre. Or else."

"Or else?"

"Or else you, too, won't live beyond this day."

CHAPTER TWENTY-TWO

"WHY DID YOU put me in this dilemma?" I asked Stuart.

The gamers slowly marched him to the room where they'd end his life.

"Tayler, you met my supervisor before I even knew he was a tin man. This is as weird for me as it is for you."

"But you could have let me and Carter fix this place. Why do you fight against restoring humanity? You do it continually. For goodness' sake, Stuart, the world does not revolve around you and your narcissistic ambition."

The gamers' stomping feet rebounded down the hall. A clear indication no one was around. Their armoured suits as imposing as the robot without a soul.

Stuart's shoes shuffled while I toddled along, reading his face for a sign of regret.

"You are obsessed with me," I said.

"You show up and the world loves you," he replied. "I show up and I have to prove myself."

"But look at the cost. You control societies outside their natural order, or you contribute to their shortcomings. You did it in Astra City. You went along with it in Beta City. You must know you're not on the side that can win." I tried to halt the gamers, but they kept walking. "Why do you think the world loves me?"

"Oh, come on now! Once you fell in with the social media socialites, you were one of Astra City's favourite influencers. And here in Beta City, you vlog and the public goes apeshit for more of you. No one's given me the affection you get naturally just for showing up."

"You *are* obsessed with me." I stood still. "He is obsessed with me," I said softly to myself.

"Come on, Tayler. You know you have to watch my execution. Otherwise, you'll be next."

I followed. "Someone must have loved you."

"Not the way they love you."

"But someone must have. Your mum. Your dad. A girl. Someone loved you at some stage."

"My parents loved me as much as anyone gaining love from the online masses. They blogged as if their life depended on it. As if the world would crumble if people didn't approve of their posts. And I read those posts when I was old enough. And those posts were never about me or their parenting skills with little man Stuart. They were about boring things."

"Like what?"

"Like a rainbow they saw on a morning walk. Like the

dog that followed them home one day. Like the shade of green of the grass after the rain. But. Nothing. About. Their. Son."

I grabbed his arm. "Listen." The gamers pointed their guns at me. "My parents were more interested in their social media posts than in me, and I hated it. I lost my childhood to the almighty Social Media Central. But I didn't try to rule the world like a sociopath punishing everyone through the very tool that distracted my parents. You are responsible for what is happening to you. Not me. Not your parents." The gamers pulled him away from my grip. Their death march continued. "Stuart, you must see that."

"You're a giver, Tayler. You make the mistake takers like me never make. You give because you don't know when to stop. You give as long as takers keep taking."

"But look at you. You gave and gave to a robotic taker."

A door slid open. They scuffled Stuart inside. There was no furniture. Just a couple of ropes and concrete walls splattered with dried blood.

"I'm about to die."

"Is there anyone I need to give a message to?"

"Tayler." He chuckled. "Little boy Tayler who wanders past a stranger and finds an instant friend, no one will care if I die. No past lover. No bosom buddy. No former employer. No youthful nemesis. No, Tayler, my death won't even be worthy of a post. No one will care."

"Little man Stuart, someone will care."

They tied his wrists with the hanging rope. The door slid shut. I stayed outside. Even with the threat of my own demise if I didn't watch and report back to the robot, I couldn't. It would haunt me forever.

He screamed like an animal slaughtered for food. The deafening shots drumrolled his demise. A silence followed as if mourners were gathered and quietly reflecting. But I was the only one grieving.

I heard the untying of the ropes and the slump of his body. My eyes stung. The door slid open, and the sound of efficient soldiers dragging someone they deemed worthless made me choke. I coughed through my tears, too sick to watch Stuart being put out with the garbage.

My short breaths were audible, like jagged hiccups trying to stop me crying. But cry I did. My nemesis was dead, yet my emotions bubbled like volcanic pools.

I first met Stuart on a park bench. He seemed friendly until I ran into him again and realised he'd orchestrated an elaborate plan. A plan where I'd learn heartache in the midst of deadly chaos. A plan that caused the death of a friend because she was in the way.

So why was I wailing over him? I really didn't know. Was there something more in this power play I didn't see? A touch of evil I'd become addicted to?

My weeping changed. Another reality unfolded. A robot was my boss. An artificially intelligent assassin in control of the minds of the citizens. Teasing them through fake posts and comments to alter their lives. The ultimate game of cat and mouse.

I wiped my cheeks with the bottom of my shirt. My breaths were still short, but no sound came from my larynx. This expansive compound felt as restrictive as a prison cell. I shut my eyes. No. I could see the robot in my mind. I opened my eyes. Still no one around.

Do I run? It sees everything. Where are the cameras?

I wandered listlessly in the direction of my fate. Total control under the tin man with unwanted observations. I stopped and considered sneaking to the exit. Those militarised gamers could come from anywhere. Look where my good-for-nothing need to help the people of Beta City landed me. Why did I let Carter talk me into this?

"Tayler!" Sage had returned and was sprinting towards me.

"Run!" I yelled. "It sees everything." I bolted to my lover. "Just go. Don't wait for me. I'm right behind you."

Several emojis appeared on parts of the wall. Hidden speakers broadcasted "I see you, little boy Tayler, whose sugar is so sweet the hordes fight for a taste."

"Who *is* that anyway?" Sage yelled.

"The freakiest AI you'll ever meet. Now, run!"

Swoosh. A bullet shot past my ear. *Woosh*. Another almost grazed my leg.

Sage was out of sight. I wasn't far behind. The exit was near. More bullets, but I was out of their reach.

Fresh air. Our bus purred, ready to escape. Carter beckoned me to hurry. Sage rushed up the steps and to the back seat. Bullets smashed a window. The robot stood like a general, urging the gamers to charge at us. Its cannon-like arms pushed them forward, but their clumsy armour made them stumble onto the gravel. They got to their feet.

Carter pressed the accelerator and we stormed ahead. We soon lost them.

"What's that sound?" Hudson peered out of a broken window, being careful not to cut herself on the broken glass left in the frame.

The gamers rode space-age hoverboards. Zooming

through the air with the skill of surfers on a wave.

"Duck!" Hudson hollered.

More shattered glass. Another glassless window.

"Go faster, man," Sage yelled.

"My foot's to the floor!" Carter weaved, causing Hudson to clutch the window frame and slice her thumb on the broken shards.

Sage held my head to his chest. My heart raced, but my mind was frazzled from emotional overload. He stroked my temple then played with my hair, curling a few strands.

More shattered glass. More gunfire. And me, blocking out enough to keep me sane, but not enough to lose my grip on the danger we were in.

CHAPTER TWENTY-THREE

"HEAD TO CRADLE Edge," I hollered.

"Why?" Hudson asked.

Another bullet smashed another window.

"Trust me," I replied. "I'll explain later."

The armoured gamers caught up, hoverboarding at opposite sides of our bus. One carefully clutched the frame of a shattered window. One foot balanced on his flying contraption as his other foot raised to the level of the frame. Sage charged, determined to push him out before he could enter our vehicle. The other gamer raised his gun.

I jumped at Sage and knocked him to the floor. The shot was fired. The gamer who tried to enter was struck. His body thrown to the ground like a cigarette butt.

I rushed at the other one, but as he took aim, I leaped out of the way and onto the floor. He shifted his aim. I sprung up, but as I did, Carter turned the bus. I lost my balance and landed on my arm.

Both Sage and I picked at the glass fragments that hung from our skin while Carter kept erratically changing the direction of our bus.

"The other one's dead," Hudson said.

We looked. She was right.

"We're almost out of power." Carter's voice wavered. "Shit. The fuel gauge just turned red."

Every time the gamer steered himself to the side of our bus, Carter manoeuvred to keep him in view of the driver's window. He aimed at Carter, but our vehicle sped up, spreading our attacker like a bug on a truck's radiator guard.

"Jump out of the bus!" Carter opened the doors.

"What?" Hudson glared at him.

"Jump out of the bus." Carter glanced back at us. "Now!"

Sage clutched my arm and scuttled to the door. He half smiled at me, then counted to three. The multiple cuts on our bare skin were now chafed by gravel as we bounced like stones skimming on a river.

Hudson somersaulted out of the door, prize-winning gymnast style. Sage also saw her graceful exit, then turned to me with the embarrassed look of the acrobat who didn't make the team.

The gamer slid sideways, attempting to escape the inertia of the vehicle. But Carter was speeding towards a road sign. With one almighty smash, force met the stationary object. We carefully rose. Aches and pains accompanied our desire to get a better look at what just happened.

The dust settled. The gamer's battered armour lay on

the dirt behind the bus. We weren't sure if the might of impact killed him, or if falling from the window and being run over sealed his fate.

The front of our vehicle was a twisted wreck. Carter groaned. We stepped through the back door. Carter was gripping the rear ledge of the bus from the back seat.

"You can let go now," I said. "He's dead."

Carter let out a slow moan.

"He's in shock," Hudson said.

A helicopter flew overhead.

"Quick. Duck!" I yelled. "Before they see us."

Carter was still cemented to the chair like a visitor to a haunted manor who'd just seen the ghost. We reached up, gripped his arms, and guided him to the floor. We all crouched so more glass fragments couldn't pierce our skin.

We waited. The spy in the sky moved on ahead, eventually.

"It's aware its soldiers are dead," I muttered.

"By 'it', you mean the robot that watched us escape?" Hudson's face had a lighter shade.

I nodded. "The ultimate artificial intelligence. It controls Social Media Central, creating fake posts and different versions of feeds that are fed to different people."

"A robot does that?" Sage furrowed a brow. "Why can't software do that?"

"Because that robot was a prototype of Stage Three." I motioned to everyone to leave the bus. "They've built androids to fool people who don't use Social Media Central." We wandered outside. I gazed at the sky. "In fact, maybe that helicopter…"

"What is it, Tayler?" Carter was coming back to life.

"Maybe that helicopter is taking Audrey to Cradle Edge."

"Who's Audrey?" Hudson asked.

I faced Carter. "Remember Frederica?"

"Who?" Sage asked.

"A friend of ours at Cradle Edge," Carter replied. "Tayler and I were at the Unicorn Hotel with Frederica and Ralph before this crazy adventure began."

"Frederica is an android." It sounded silly, even as I said it.

"A what?" Carter stared at me, as if questioning my sanity.

"Frederica is influencing her friends at Cradle Edge. Audrey is another android on her way to fool people who believe Social Media Central has no effect on them."

The others halted. Their open mouths nearly swallowed flies.

"I'm serious," I said. "I don't know how many androids have infiltrated Cradle Edge, but that society isn't free from the clutches of mind control. Eventually the World Bank will change it to another Beta City."

They all exchanged glances.

"We have to get to Cradle Edge as quickly as possible. I know I sound crazy. I know this whole plan sounds crazy, but that's what Stage Three is. Influence through contact."

"What do we do when we get there?" Sage's tender grin let me know he believed me.

"I don't know." I shook my head. "I really don't know. But we have a long walk ahead. We have plenty of time to come up with a plan."

"IS THAT A gun in my back or are you just happy to see me?" I said to Sage. I was piggybacking him.

"It's a gun, man. I took it from the crushed augmented reality player."

"When?"

He kissed the top of my head. "I'm joking."

It was a day after Carter smashed our bus. He was piggybacking Hudson who piggybacked him earlier that day. They were ahead of us.

"Cradle Edge." Sage read the sign that indicated our destination was close.

My feet ached, but I wanted to carry Sage. He didn't sleep well on the patch of dried grass we lay on the night before. The bags under his eyes were more like luggage.

"I don't mind walking. I must be heavy." Sage kissed the top of my head again.

"You'll never be a burden." I surprised myself with my reply. *How soppy.*

Regardless, he jumped off my back. His smirk was schmaltzier than my last words to him.

"Don't give me that look," I said.

"What look?"

"The look that says after all we've been through, like..."

"Like me holding you to my chest, Tayler, in the backseat of the bus. Like you piggybacking me. Like your sexual remark about a gun in my pocket."

I halted. "What am I to you, Sage?" I then realised there was no time for this conversation. We were on a mission. I kept walking.

"You're really asking that question, man?"

"Yes, I'm really asking that question, *man.*"

"Love scares you."

"Tell me something I don't know."

"I'm not Madeline Q."

The man I once met with the faraway gaze was now the man determined to get under my skin. His touch felt good. His sly smirks made me smile instantly. Even the nose ring I thought was an unneeded blemish to his face adorned him with character. Oh, I'd fallen.

"Tayler, you're still looking at me like I scare you."

"I'm not."

"If I had a mirror..."

"I really don't think you're Madeline Q."

"I'm sassier."

"Well, not really."

"You haven't seen me in full flight." Sage moved towards me.

"You're expecting a kiss, aren't you?"

"Maybe. Let your guard down."

"I've been burnt."

"Why would I deceive you?" He puckered his lips.

And there it was. The question I didn't have a rational answer for.

"Hey, guys!" Carter yelled. "Look."

The helicopter had landed outside the city, far enough away so no one would know Audrey was a visitor.

"We still don't have a plan." Carter kept our gaze until we caught up to him.

"Ask Tayler," Sage declared. "He has all the answers." Another sly smirk was aimed at me. I didn't smile back.

"What's that supposed to mean?" Hudson asked.

"Nothing." Sage held my hand. "Nothing Tayler thinks is worth explaining."

CHAPTER TWENTY-FOUR

I LEAPED ONTO a table, disturbing the patrons at the Unicorn Hotel. I scanned the room to find either Audrey or Frederica. Neither was here.

"You should say something while you're up there," Hudson insisted.

I crouched. "I was going to, but what if other androids are here?"

"Everyone's looking at you. Now's the time to warn them."

"We should have come up with a plan." I stood and waved timidly. "Hi, I'm Tayler and I need to tell you something." Sage gave me a reassuring nod. "Artificial Intelligence powered by Social Media Central has infiltrated Cradle Edge. In the form of androids."

Laughter filled the pub. Hudson joined me on the table.

"He's right," she said. "An android named Audrey has landed on the outskirts."

Louder giggles. One polite customer asked us to step down.

"I know this sounds crazy," I said. "I know it sounds like fiction but believe me, I've seen her. She's here. She's designed to infiltrate your lives and direct the way you think."

"As long as she can make a cocktail, I'm not worried," a stocky man shouted over the mirth-filled chatter.

The barman marched over to us, pointing downwards to the polished floorboards. I moved to get down, but Hudson grabbed my arm.

"Don't you understand," she yelled. "You're not safe anymore. This last haven from Social Media Central is no longer a haven!"

The barman tapped his fingers on our table. Hudson and I came down. The barman led us on a walk of shame. Taunts were aimed at us, and the way some stared you'd have thought we just ate their children.

Someone nudged my chest. I kept walking so this same person patted my shoulder. I turned and faced an older man with sculpted white hair. "There's no internet infrastructure here," he said. "SMC can't touch us."

"There has to be," I replied. "The infrastructure has been built. I know because I met one of the SMC androids here in this pub."

"It's true," Carter retorted. "I know the woman Tayler's talking about. And we've seen the robot who was the prototype. He's impressive. Trust me. This evil plan has been in the works for a while, well beyond anyone's gaze."

"I suspected, but I didn't believe..." We waited for the old man to finish. His eyes were misty. He gazed blankly into the distance, like a scientist retracing his steps to work out why his experiment failed. "Where are you taking them?" he asked the barman.

"To the manager. She's out the back."

"I'm coming with them," he answered. "This is an important conversation."

Crash!

The front door blew inwards, knocking several punters to the floor. Small flames licked the door frame, which was already burnt black. Panicked patrons huddled at the opposite end of the room. A few lent a hand to those on the polished floorboards, dragging them away from danger as quickly as they could.

Then she appeared, standing like a leather-clad supervillain from an old movie. Her tight-fitting one-piece was not an outfit for blending in. It was worn to make a statement. A statement of superiority. A statement of "hell has just arrived".

Two armoured gamers joined her, ray guns to the ready. No simple bullets for this crowd. This was no longer a subtle takeover of minds. This was a demonstration of authoritarian power.

Sage yelled, "Sleep now." The gamers looked his way. So did many patrons. He turned to me and claimed, "Well, it was worth a try."

"Is this Sabastian's lair?" the shorter gamer asked.

"Is this what?" someone questioned.

"Don't be fooled," replied the other gamer. "Sabastian has several lairs. The question is whether this is where we find Sabastian."

"Who is Sabastian?" someone else called out.

"It doesn't matter," I yelled. "They're inside an augmented reality game."

"Isn't that the Enemy Alien?" the short gamer asked. He pointed his gun at me.

"You'll have your fun later," Audrey explained. Her alluring voice could have seduced a dead man. "It's my turn to have fun." She moved forward, then gestured to her henchmen to stay where they were. "When I choose, you shoot."

A small stream of people found their way to the back room where the manager was. She came out.

"Stop them," Audrey called to her. "They mustn't escape or else I'll get my boys to aim in their direction." As the sinister android strode, it was apparent she wore heels. Each step was in perfect time, like the ticking of a clock. Her makers appreciated quality engineering.

"Who are you and why are you in my pub?" the manager demanded.

Audrey reached for her own chin, wriggled her face, and snapped it off. Lights and multi-coloured wires revealed how lifeless she was to the patrons. "I'm your superior," she said from the mouth on her face still in her hand. She clicked it back in place.

That nice old man looked down in despair. Some gasped while others turned pale. The manager was stiff, as if turned to stone. The barman waved his hand in front of her, but her shock was too great. She fainted with a huge *clump*.

Audrey strutted into the crowd, then halted, studied the patrons, and grabbed a man by his collar. She eased his face to hers. "Ever fantasised about having sex with a machine? A vacuum cleaner? A massage tool, perhaps?"

The man shook his head so fast his neck cracked.

"Pity," Audrey continued. "I'll have my men shoot you if you don't enjoy what I'm about to do. Now kneel!"

She forced him to the ground. His knees whacked the floor.

"Feel my legs," she commanded. "I said 'Feel my legs'."

He rubbed her. The leather on her body squeaked.

"Be forceful, you stupid organic lifeform. I want nails!"

He ran his short fingernails against her. She moaned before cackling like a mad scientist.

"You'll live." She kicked him away.

The girl the man landed on squealed. She stared in fear. Sweat formed under her arms, staining her white blouse. She tightened her lips.

"What's your name, you pretty thing?" Audrey's voice tormented her silence.

"Camille." She choked on her answer.

"Louder. What is your name?"

"Camille." Her volume increased slightly.

"Why does the race that rules the planet fear losing control, Camille?"

"I don't know."

"Well, you must have some insight into it. You're shaking like a leaf in a storm." Audrey snickered. "Tell me, dear sweet Camille, what are you so afraid of?"

"You."

"Congratulations. That's the right answer. You get to live."

The patrons in front of the crowd wormed their way

back. Some even pulled those behind to the front. Audrey noticed. Her hand shot away from her arm, yet it stayed connected by a metallic cord. She grabbed one of those retreating and dragged him back to her. Her hand snapped back at her wrist.

"This is Sabastian," she said to her soldiers.

The taller gamer fetched him, took him back to the entrance, and held him in place even as he tried to run.

Audrey held the gaze of an older woman with frizzy hair. Her blue coat was the same hue as her eyes.

"You're not scared of me." Audrey gestured to the short gamer. Like a loyal puppy, he came to her side. "You're a fan of the symbiotic relationship between man and machine?"

"I could be, but today is not the day I want to find out."

"You're a brave organic, talking back to the machine that could end your life."

My heart thumped through my chest. Sage clutched my hand tight. This was too horrible to watch and too intense to look away from.

The frizzy-haired woman strolled up to Audrey and the gamer. "If your soldiers didn't have weapons, would you still believe you're superior?"

"There are many things that make me superior. The fact that my limbs detach and snap back in place. The fact that my intellect is ever increasing as more fools around the country live and breathe Social Media Central, my personal neural network."

"But you don't know any of us. We've shunned SMC."

"True. That makes you in some way superior to your fellow organics from the cities, even if you haven't grasped SMC's reach here in Cradle Edge. But does it make you superior to me?" Audrey rested her finger on her cheek. "I don't think so."

"Intellect comes from human experience, and human curiosity. Not from the rantings and baseless opinions being fed into your neural network."

"I like you. You challenge me. You're delicious in your own way." The android shared a sinister glance with her gamer. "Kill her."

He grabbed her by her coat, held her in place, and took aim. Several screamed. Some yelled, "Stop!" But no one moved.

Sage pressed me close to his side. It was clear he understood when I wasn't coping. Of all the things I could have thought about at that moment, my boyfriend's ability to read me pulled focus.

Hudson and Carter stood near the gentle man with the chiselled hairdo. He reached for their hands, his kindness permeating through the insanity.

Audrey smirked like a politician who'd gotten away with a lie. "Now!" she barked.

One flash of golden light and the evil deed was done. The wisdom of an older woman snuffed out in a town where the rules had changed. But there were weird murmurs around the rising smoke where her body had been.

I lunged forward. Sage moved with me. He gasped first. I stared. I glanced at Sage. I looked again, but still I couldn't believe what I was seeing.

CHAPTER TWENTY-FIVE

AN ELECTRICAL MESS was melted on the floorboards. The frizzy-haired woman was no organic. Her charred remains smoked like an outdated toaster burning the bread. And she buzzed loudly as her once internal lights struggled to stay lit.

"What the..." uttered a woman with pink hair.

"Who else is a robot?" asked a guy in a nap-shirt.

"Whoever that wiry-haired android was, she developed a conscience," Carter said.

"I know," I replied.

"Yeah," Hudson added. "She sacrificed herself to save a human."

"The effect of living with people in Cradle Edge." I studied Audrey, wondering if there was a way to conform her.

"Who else can I play with?" Audrey's heels stomped in

perfect time once again, as she scrutinised the patrons with a menacing smirk. Her short henchman followed. She eventually settled on a young man with wire-framed glasses. "You look good. You're too dumbfounded not to be an organic."

"Are you the keeper of the Hyena's mirth?" Sage called out to the soldier by her side.

"The Hyena's mirth has been stolen by ninjas loyal to the space-travelling nun," he replied.

"The space-travelling nun plays Scrabble for money," the other gamer disclosed. "She gave the ninjas cash to buy the Hyena's mirth, so technically the mirth wasn't stolen."

"What the hell are they talking about?" a confused patron asked.

"Are any of them trapped in Sabastian's lair?" I asked.

"No, my friend." He let go of the man he was keeping captive by the door. The man cautiously crept outside. "Sabastian's lair is a construct. A place still to be built."

"I thought Sabastian had several lairs," Hudson stated.

Audrey stomped her foot. "You're supposed to focus on me!"

"Could the hyena's mirth be used to build Sabastian's lair?" a random patron asked. "One laugh could dig into a cave. Another giggle could conjure up designer furniture."

"Then the space-travelling nun and the ninjas can have a hangout, if Sabastian doesn't mind flatmates." The girl with pink hair feigned seriousness.

"The nun and the ninjas could be like Snow White and her dwarfs," the older man near us said. "Does the nun rely on the ninjas more than buying Hyena mirth?"

"Men!" Audrey stomped her foot once more, getting her

heel caught between floorboards. "Stop answering their questions." She was losing balance.

"The nun is comforted by the Hyena's mirth, which she wears like a fur coat," the gamer near Audrey replied. "It kept her warm on Europa."

"Europa?" someone asked.

"It's one of Jupiter's—"

Clunk! Audrey fell to the floor while desperately trying to free her heel. Patrons swarmed her and held her down. One person wrapped his handkerchief around her mouth. Her gagged murmurs got the attention of the gamers. The one at the door raised his ray gun.

"What's Sabastian like?" someone yelled out to him.

He lowered his gun. "You know, I don't like his girl-friend."

The person who asked about Sabastian sidled up to the gamer and placed her arm around his shoulder. "Why don't you like his girlfriend?"

"She takes baths on Tuesdays and showers on Wednesdays. It's her pattern. I suspect she's too clean on those days, and less clean on others."

"Can I buy you a drink?" The patron gestured to the bar.

"I can't take off my mask."

"That's okay. You can watch me drink."

The barman rushed back to his post, got her a drink, and joined the inane conversation.

Others kept the short gamer occupied with queries about the nun. This led to a discussion about a spiritual guru who once accompanied her to Saturn.

Some patrons examined the charred remains of the frizzy-haired android, who no longer showed signs of life.

One long-haired guy nudged the melted metallic skeleton with his shoe, causing what was left of her arm to detach and thud to the ground.

Someone raised their hand from the crowd gathered around Audrey, who was still thrashing while the horde pinned her down. I then realised the someone with their hand in the air was holding a shiny piece of metal. It was Audrey's face. He flung it. Another caught it. Her mouth still moved as she demanded they stop, but it kept being frisbeed from patron to patron.

For some reason, the crowd huddled closer, tightening their makeshift cage around the android. But they were forced apart. Audrey stood and it was clear by the sound of her heels, she was no longer stuck. As they moved in again to keep her contained, she let her hand fly once more and wrapped a tall blond guy with her metallic cord.

"Make one move and I'll squeeze this man to death." Her voice still came from her dismounted mouth which was now sitting on the bar. She gripped him tighter. He gasped for breath. "Who's going to bring my face back? Someone? Anyone?"

"Help me," the blond guy wheezed.

The barman strode towards Audrey with her face. "Let him go and you can have this." He waved it like a fan.

She clutched the man tighter. He struggled to breathe. Then we were blinded by another blazing golden light.

The barman shot off her head. He had taken the ray gun the gamer chatting at the bar once held and hid it behind his back as he approached her. Flapping her face was a distraction.

The blond man passed out as the deathly grip was

loosened. People gave him air while someone fetched a glass of water.

Unlike the other molten android, Audrey didn't liquefy. She stood like a manikin without a head. A testament to the craftsmanship of her makers and a warning that these robots had been built and finessed over time. More time than we imagined. The stench of her scorched rubber collar irritated me.

Sage yelled out, "Now sleep." The gamers instantly dropped.

I kissed my boyfriend.

The motionless players were dragged behind the bar. Carter and Hudson helped. Everyone struggled with the weight of their armour, causing the floor to be scratched by the sharper edges of the metal.

"Tayler, are you okay?" Sage asked.

I nodded. "I feel like my brain is exploding from all the weirdness."

"Restless robots. Sabastian's lair. It's like a black-and-white movie, man, where a scientist is trying to warn the citizens of impending doom, but no one is listening."

"There was no scientist in this scenario. Even Stuart Manning had no idea his boss was a robot."

"Are we safe?"

I searched for an answer. "Only if the androids already in this crowd have developed a conscience like…" I gestured to the smelted android who stood up to Audrey.

"Everyone seems to be on our side. So, if there's an android or two in here, they're helping the humans."

I held Sage close. While patrons prodded Audrey or bonded over a drink to make sense of this ordeal, I cuddled my boyfriend.

Something crashed to the ground. A chunk of Audrey's circuitry had loosened and was on display for everyone to study. The barman found an axe and started hacking off her arms.

"It's a robot, man," Sage reminded me. "Stop screwing up your face as if they're butchering a person."

He held my chin and brought my lips to his. Another kiss to remind me what my priorities were. Another dreamy trance to lose myself in. Another tickle from his goatee to bring me back to reality.

He was my solace from now on, no matter where we were.

CHAPTER TWENTY-SIX

THE FOLLOWING MORNING, they placed Audrey in the front garden of the Unicorn Hotel, draping vines around her to create a work of art. As I viewed this lifeless machine, I feared the next android attack.

The night before, we checked ourselves into a motel. Hudson and Carter shared a room with two single beds to save money. Sage and I splurged on a room with a queen-sized bed. We all looked forward to some much-needed rest.

"We have to contact Vanessa," Carter said. He and Hudson were in our room. "Or Sonya. We have to warn them about the androids."

"If they're still alive," Hudson replied. She reached inside her leather jacket.

"How do we contact them without using Social Media

Central?" I wrapped my arm around Sage who was sitting on the bed with me. "Unless we can send a carrier pigeon, their goose is cooked."

"Nice play on words." Sage kissed me.

"I think I'm going to be sick." Hudson rolled her eyes.

"Sorry, Edelweiss." I smirked. "What does that mean anyway? Was that your lovey-dovey name for Vanessa?"

She took off her jacket and reached inside. "Now's not the time to explain it."

"True." Carter paced, leaving dirt on the aged carpet. "We need to speak to the manager."

"Are we recruiting the manager now?" Hudson asked. She shook her jacket.

"No," Carter replied. "A motel needs to communicate outside of town. How else do they get visitors? The manager might be able to contact our friends."

"I'll talk to her." Sage was stopped by Carter before he reached the door.

"We should all go," Carter said.

"No," I replied. "Sage and I will go. We can't all storm that poor woman's office. Carter, you're overanxious at the moment—"

"Can you blame me? After metal-crazed Audrey and her bloodthirsty henchmen?"

"Sabastian picked the wrong lair," Hudson said, smugly. She patted her jean pockets.

"Again, nice play on words," Sage replied. "Have you lost your vaper?"

She nodded. "We all need a puff. Especially Carter. Where is that damn thing?"

"When did you last see it?" I asked.

Hudson shrugged. "Carter, we need a shot of bourbon or vodka, or anything to calm our nerves. Let's go to the bar. Sage and Tayler can fill us in later."

"But we need to talk to Vanessa and Sonya." Carter stayed adamant.

"And that's what Sage and Tayler intend to do. For all our sakes."

"She's right, man. If you don't have a drink, you won't sleep tonight. You have no idea where that vaper is?"

She shook her head.

"What was in your tobacco?" Carter asked.

"Something for cramps. But it was a nice high."

"I can ask the manager if she has a joint," I said. "She looks fairly hippy. Or we'll find a chemist to get us all some sleeping pills."

Carter closed his eyes. "Anything will do. The killer android concept has fried my brain. Now I know how you felt, Tayler, when you met that robot."

I nodded, then asked him to sit on the bed with me. I massaged his shoulders for a minute or two before Hudson took over.

"Better?" she asked.

"Better," Carter replied. "Tayler, Sage, go and find out what you can. I don't need another escapade. Well, not now, anyway." He glanced over his shoulder at Hudson. "A little harder above the collarbone."

"It will turn up when you're not looking for it," I said.

"Do you vape on the loo?" Sage asked. "It could be there."

Hudson pondered as we headed for the office. The jovial manager was munching an éclair while smearing chocolate all over her sticky fingers.

"Have one," she said. There was an assortment of cakes on a plate on her desk. Lemon cupcakes with white frosting. Jam-filled doughnuts. Two more éclairs. "I've been baking all afternoon. It's what I do when I'm nervous. Bake and eat. Eat and bake."

"Why are you nervous?" Sage asked. But as he looked at the ceiling, I knew he'd worked out why.

"You didn't hear about the killer army at the Unicorn Hotel? It was a slaughterhouse."

"It wasn't that bad," I said.

"How would you know?"

"We were there," Sage replied.

"If you're that scared, why didn't you shut the motel and leave?" I took a cupcake.

"I really don't know. I was going to. Then I wasn't. Then I baked. Then I ate. Then I was too scared to leave."

"There were two killer soldiers, but they're in custody," Sage explained. "And the android short circuited."

"The android?" She accidentally squished her éclair.

"Yeah, an android," I said. "No one got killed at the pub, except for another android, but…"

"What's the matter?" Sage asked me.

"Nothing. Yeah, it's nothing."

"It's obviously something," the manager replied. "You're talking about androids and killer soldiers. It's something."

Sage rubbed my back. I composed myself. I couldn't risk freaking her out more if I was going to reach our friends. She grabbed a tissue and did her best to wipe the cream and chocolate from her hand.

"By the way, I'm Tayler, and this is my boyfriend, Sage."

"Your boyfriend," Sage repeated, cheerfully.

"I'm Lilly-Of-The-Valley. Lilly for short." She shook both our hands. "Now tell me more about these androids."

"Shortly," I replied. "We have a couple of friends in Beta City, and we were wondering if there was a way to reach them."

She peered at me like a detective deciding if I was friend or foe. Then she invited us behind the desk and grabbed two garden chairs from her storeroom.

She lifted a door to a compartment on her desk, revealing an old computer with a greenish screen.

"Too many guests can't detach themselves from Social Media Central, so I hide this contraption."

Lilly turned it on, then picked up the phone and dialled the operator. "Margaret, link me through to...Tayler, you did say Beta City?" I nodded. "Link me through to Beta City's SMC."

"So, you know about the different versions of Social Media Central?" I asked her.

"Yep. I have guests from all over the country with different versions of history, news, everything."

I didn't dare tell her the android attack yesterday was because SMC was already operating at Cradle Edge. I didn't want to think about it myself.

A strange collection of beeps and screeches came from her computer.

"Thank you, Margaret." Lilly hung up.

"How do people book to stay if...?" I wasn't exactly sure what I was asking.

"Yes, Tayler, I have a website, but its infrastructure is in

Cradle Edge's telecommunications office. People can look at rooms but have to call the number on the home page to reach me. That number calls the operator who connects me."

"That seems inconvenient." Sage examined a doughnut.

"It's how life is meant to be." Lilly pulled out a drawer and reached for a joint. After she lit it, she offered us a toke. I waved it away. Sage looked at me, surprised, but he did the same. Then she pulled out a book and showed us its pages full of handwritten entries.

"It will take a while for this old thing to connect, so in the meantime, I will read to you." She pulled a pair of thin wire-frame spectacles and eased them onto her face with the care a monarch takes putting on a crown. "Sage, this is my great-aunt's diary. This is how life is meant to be."

Lilly cleared her throat. "The problem with the internet is it connected stupid people." And so, she began. She read how as a child long before the internet was invented, people would visit her great-aunt's parents' house randomly for a chat, so a spare packet of biscuits and plenty of teabags were always kept in the pantry. About how people shared in robust political debates and continued to do this when the internet first came to be. People loved changing the minds of others as much as they loved having their own mind changed. It was the true definition of communication. Then, at around the time videos of cats doing funny things became popular, people got angry when political posts were published.

Her great-aunt noticed those around her were no longer interested in politics. They now saw the opposing political parties as competitors in a sports match. It didn't matter if the government held secret trials to jail whistle-blowers. Or if refugees were held in offshore detention indefinitely. Or if a family were plucked from their country town to also be imprisoned overseas. Or if the country's economic deficit had been doubled but the Prime Minister (I thought this was a quaint phrase when I heard it) claimed otherwise.

"As long as their party won," Lilly said. "That's all that mattered."

"When did a Prime Minister become the Government?" I asked.

"When anyone who remembered the lessons of the Second World War—"

"The second world what?" Sage asked.

"A war that taught future generations the importance of standing up for what's right," Lilly replied. "A lesson forgotten when too much conflicting information existed on the internet, so some changed their reality, then fought with those who never did."

"That's when a Prime Minister became the Government?" Sage decided to smoke a little of the joint.

"Not long after. I've read my great-aunt's diary hundreds of times. It's my only real history book. I laugh to myself when guests tell me the history of the world. Their Social Media Central history of the world. I know otherwise. I have a real history book."

"You admire her." I waved away the joint when Sage offered it.

"She was young when people believed in science. When people read the news or watched someone presenting it before the days when federal authorities stormed the homes of journalists who'd done their jobs too well."

"On a TV," I said.

"You know what a TV is?"

I nodded. "Did people care about things in the age of TV?"

"Yes," she replied. "Many still cared in the age of the internet too. Good things were done through the internet. But the mood changed, eventually. Or rather, the internet changed people's moods."

"Sounds like the internet changed people's values." Sage's eyes were glazed.

"Not my great-aunt's. She held on to the values her parents taught her, even when her parents abandoned them."

"Isn't that democracy?" Sage's stoner musing was lost on us. "Man, like, when the whole world is speaking to each other, we all move forward."

Lilly opened the diary to a bookmarked page and read.

"People were so glad to find their online tribe, they relished what made them the same as those people, rather than finding what similarities they had with the people physically around them. Online became their happy place.

"Yet we all learned what we could say to whichever group of people we were with when the internet didn't exist. My sewing group had a different set of values to the friends who I cooked for. Ideas were shared and challenged, then further shared and challenged in different social situations, in line with what the etiquette was for that particular group.

"But internet forums gave everyone a misplaced sense of bravado. There was no room for shades of grey in an argument. People no longer dealt in facts. They found opinions to help create the reality they wanted, then either agreed with you or not, leaving the art of critical thinking for dead. Until the virus."

"Why did you stop?" I asked Lilly. "Your great-aunt's diary is fascinating."

She showed me where she was up to. It was the last page.

"Don't ask me what the virus was." Lilly closed the diary. "She didn't write anything about it. My great-aunt started another diary much later in life. And I have to tell you this bit. A social media platform was forced to close by the Prime Minister. She said it was favoured by writers, teachers...intellectuals in general. The Prime Minister didn't like being critiqued so he passed legislation to shut it down."

"Passed legislation?" Sage asked.

"I don't know what that means either, but this social media platform fought back. It created its own mobile phones."

"Mobile phones?" Sage was struggling to follow.

"It's what SMC devices were called a long time ago," I explained.

"Anyway, they affiliated with software companies that shared their values so their mobile phones carried bookshops, dating sites, and whatever else appealed to people with the same mindset."

"What does the diary say about Social Media Central?" I asked.

"It didn't exist when she was alive. I wish it did. I'd love to know what she'd think of it." Lilly beamed. "There's one more thing I need to share. My great-aunt was horrified some religious organisation called The Vatican created its own cryptocurrency, then worked hard with leaders around the world to reduce the wages of the working class, while promising those leaders great returns on Vatcoin. It bankrupted richer nations at a time when poorer nations were already bankrupt."

"Entrepreneurship," I mumbled. "The Radical Faith Alliance. That's the context. Religion and employment are one."

Sage stared at me for a very long time. No one spoke. The whirr of the ceiling fan was evident. I was unsettled. I wanted to travel in time and meet Lilly-Of-The-Valley's great-aunt and see what she saw for myself. Make sense of it. Or try to.

Then I wanted to go back further in time. To watch TV. To see a time when values were held high, and everyone shared the same information.

The computer made more mysterious beeps, as if it was talking to itself. A logo was distorting on the screen. Lilly swivelled on her chair and reached for the window. She opened it and turned a rod that was just outside. I peered out to see the huge antenna which she was rotating. The image on the screen settled to display a white SMC logo on a murky green background. She closed the window.

"Who do you need to contact?" she asked.

"She's called Vanessa," Sage replied. "She runs a vlog."

Lilly-Of-The-Valley passed the plate of cakes to him. Sage chomped into another doughnut. She typed "Vanessa", "Vlog", "Beta City".

Several images of different women and one man filled the screen.

"That's her." Sage pointed to our Vanessa.

Lilly clicked her image and soon we were staring at our puzzled friend in the midst of a street protest. When we explained how we reached her and who our old hippy friend was, she lifted her device to show us the hundreds of people who came out to strike. So many downtrodden faces learning to smile for the first time. Tired yet driven elders. Recharged mid-life folk finding a reason for being. And younger peeps who hadn't been in service long and knew it was wrong.

"But the vlog where I tell everyone to go on strike shouldn't be posted—"

"Until later this week." Vanessa shrugged. "We posted it early, sweetheart. After your bus was chased by hoodlums, we had to get the message out. We were scared Stuart would do something rash if we didn't take over Beta City earlier."

I kept the death of my nemesis to myself. I still had to process his demise.

"And no one came for you when we escaped?" I asked.

Vanessa shrugged again. "We didn't stay there long enough to find out. You were their target. Not us. We fled as soon as you were out of sight."

The crowd chanted behind her. She was hard to hear. A tall guy grabbed her and whisked her into the masses. She knew him. That was clear.

I yelled, "If you're in trouble, mention Sabastian's lair," but the connection cut out.

I wanted to mention the androids. I wanted to warn her so she could warn the others.

Sage gave me a stoner's wry smile. It was time to take this adventure elsewhere.

CHAPTER TWENTY-SEVEN

SAGE STOOD AGAINST the door to our room, holding the keys in his hand.

"You have to kiss me before we go in," he said.

He gazed at me as if I were a god. And although I didn't feel like one with my nagging doubts, I accepted his version of me.

We kissed.

"That's better," he said.

The muggy air brought out a scent in him that was new to me. Manly yet naïve. Dope and cotton. Clean hair and sorrow. Infatuation and need.

"I love you." My words came easily, and I meant them.

The last time I said it to him, I didn't think I'd see him again. And here with crickets chirping and a welcome breeze from time to time, the idea that I'd fallen in love didn't scare me into booking a flight for the next rocket to Mars.

He pulled me close and kissed me again. We lingered. I now knew that scent. It was Sage.

Eventually, we made it inside.

"What didn't you say to Lilly-Of-The-Valley?" He took off his shirt as he spoke.

"You're getting naked and you're asking me a question like that?"

"My man, Tayler. Avoiding the question again." He lay on top of the bedspread.

I pulled off my T-shirt. "This is going to sound crazy, but..."

"But?"

"When Stuart died, I felt all danger had passed. Yes, I met a robot, and we were chased by augmented reality losers and a sassy android named Audrey terrorised a pub. But that didn't weird me out as much as having a sociopath tie me to a roller coaster or threaten me with gelato."

"Are you sure you're not stoned?"

"I'll tell you about the gelato another time."

I unzipped my jeans, and as I was about to drop my underwear, Sage asked, "Are we boyfriends?"

"I'm sharing my inner thoughts. I wouldn't do that if—" I pulled down my underwear. "—I didn't think—" I climbed on the bed. "—there was a future in what we have."

"So, you trust me."

I gasped.

"You're saying you need as much support to make sense of the world as I do." Sage smiled.

"I guess I am."

"Now say that sentence again without 'I guess'." His wicked stoner smirk was irresistible. "I'll ask the same question, and remember, Tayler, answer 'I am'. Not 'I guess I am'. Got it?"

"Okay."

"You're saying you need as much support to make sense of the world as I do."

"I am."

"And you're saying you like it when I press your head against my chest."

"I am."

"And when I pulled shards of glass from your skin on a bus in the middle of an ambush, you liked that too."

"I did."

"And when I hear old tales of Prime Ministers with you, from hippy ladies with good weed, you like that we made a memory together."

"Yeah, we did."

"And you like it when I tell you, I was there too. You weren't the only one listening to old stories from a diary."

Oh. He was clever. I let my guard down. He was not my accessory. He was not a sexy earring or a fashionable belt.

"Sage, keep your pants on," I said. "I'm naked and I'm vulnerable. Take charge. Show me love. Keep me safe from harm."

CHAPTER TWENTY-EIGHT

MANY PATRONS FROM the previous day returned to the pub with their friends. We stood around recapping what happened because even though we all experienced it, it seemed all too bizarre to be real. Even with Audrey, lifeless, in the front garden, we needed to talk about it to prove our collective sanity.

Sage and Carter were with me. Hudson needed more time to find her tobacco tin. She was going to join us later.

I considered whether to return to Astra City or stay at Cradle Edge, a life decision that hinged on my boyfriend.

"Let's weigh up the pros and cons." Carter tapped his chin for effect. "I'm going back to Astra City, so I'll be there, Tayler. And you have other friends there."

"Including my ex-boyfriend and my ex-girlfriend," I

replied.

"I can deal with that," Sage said.

"Are you sure?" Carter asked.

"From the look on your face, I don't believe you." I held Sage's chin and playfully scrutinised his expression. "Until yesterday morning, I'd fallen in love with Cradle Edge. I saw myself living here. I still think I can."

"But Audrey and her henchmen spoiled that for you." Carter examined our drinks. "Another cider, Sage?"

"What was that?" Sage stared into space.

"I asked if you wanted another apple cider."

"No, man, that's not what I mean. Listen."

A helicopter flew overhead. A few others in the bar noticed, caught our eye, and slowly made their way outside. We did the same.

The chopper landed in a small park across from the pub. Its jet-black blades caused gusts, which rattled a child's swing. Before its android passenger jumped out, its heavily clad gamer was already playing in the park, shooting laser blasts into the air while dashing down a slide. Someone ran off in the opposite direction, but he was soon turned to ashes by the gamer's gun.

We rushed back inside with another patron, ready to warn the others. I heard one more helicopter, but I didn't look. Somehow, I thought if I didn't acknowledge it, it wouldn't be real.

Inside, two people had extended their rope-like arms and were clutching innocent customers. I realised in horror the android takeover was more advanced than we ever imagined.

I grabbed Sage and Carter and wandered cautiously

back to the front door, only to be greeted by three gamers and two metallic beings whose eyes blazed like streetlamps. One poked my chest with the force of a small hammer. I screeched.

"Who are you?" he asked. His eyes dimmed. His dark suit was a weird choice for a murderous android. Even his stylish hat made me wonder if these robots had become so advanced, they'd developed a sense of fashion. "Well, who are you, organic?"

"Tayler." I let go of Carter and touched my chest. I felt a bruise.

The android leaned closer to me. "I'm Cambridge." He turned his head to show off his alluring profile. *How can a robot be so attractive?* "Have you ever had sex with one of us, Tayler?"

"How?" I forgot I was sore. "I mean, you could damage me. Or cut my...you know...to shreds if I'm inside you."

Cambridge unbuttoned his sleeve and pushed it back. "Feel me."

I did. "You're soft." I kept stroking. "Like, really soft. What are you made from?"

He winked and rebuttoned his sleeve. "I'll tell you after we make love."

Sage pulled me sideways.

Cambridge spat, his gob landing in front of Sage's shoe. "Party pooper."

Carter shared his wide-eyed amazement. Sage's hand shook as he gripped me. Cambridge stepped towards the unsettled crowd. I crouched, reaching to see if the spit was real, but Carter jerked me back up. He gave me a stern shake of his head.

"You weren't thinking of going anywhere, Tayler?" Cambridge peered back at us. "I mean, after I play with these folks, I'll need a date. Causing mayhem is tiring for a robot like me. I need sexual healing after I claim Cradle Edge for those with vested interests."

"We should go to Astra City," Sage whispered.

"Astra City, you say?" Cambridge strolled back.

"The hyena's mirth loves Astra City." No gamer responded to Sage's sentence.

"They can't hear you," another android said. She let go of the patron she was squeezing. "You know we're all powered by Social Media Central. So, we've learned quickly from Audrey's mistake. Our soldiers don't hear what we hear."

With two killer androids focused on us, we were trapped. Other patrons watched with silent stares, too scared to stand out.

"He said 'the hyena's mirth loves Astra City'." Cambridge had raised his voice. "You see, they can't hear me. All they can hear is a separate conversation I'm sending them through my own data feed." He giggled. "I can walk and chew gum at the same time. Talk with you and talk with them, and neither you nor my little soldiers know what I'm saying to the other."

A gamer aimed at me.

"He thinks you've offended me along with the henchman who assist the travelling nun." Cambridge danced a quick jig. His agility was remarkable. "Should I tell him you've actually flattered me or intend to murder me during our sex romp later tonight?"

I tried to speak. No words came out.

He stroked my chin. "Your boyfriend is glaring at me

like a jealous husband. I might tell my soldier your boy-friend wants to murder me."

"But you're a robot," Carter reasoned. "You'd be hard to kill without a ray gun. Your henchman would know that."

"You simple-minded organic life-form, you believe they know I'm manufactured. Oh no, dearie, no. His concern is to protect the travelling nun or the hyena's mirth or what-ever nonsense I feed him. We've confused his neural net-work for so long he's lost his ability to think. Social Media Central has been reworking organic minds for generations, giving them stimuli to enjoy, or be angry about if that's what makes a stupid person feel superior. So we are masters at disconnecting organics from real life. Disconnect them from reason, and ultimately, from deeper human contact."

Cambridge turned with his arm theatrically poised in the air. The gamer still aimed at me. I pondered whether I'd be in danger while Cambridge was distracted. Surely, the gamer needed instruction, and his master was busy. Sensing what I was thinking, Sage glared at me.

"Yet you here in Cradle Edge don't have that problem." Cambridge addressed the crowd with the misdirected skill of a hammy actor. "You know the difference between an ac-quaintance and a friend. You don't burrow away agreeing with single sentence comments while attacking those whose equally simplified musings you don't agree with. And you definitely don't display this behaviour in your organic world, keeping away from people in general. You welcome having ideas open to debate."

"But that's why you're here," Carter replied. "To stop human interaction."

Cambridge raised his arms to the ceiling. Another

theatrical gesture which had us all underwhelmed before he swanned around like a king addressing his subjects.

"Yes, Carter, that's precisely what we're here to do." He looked at the gamer aiming the gun. His loyal soldier lowered his arm, keeping us safe from his trigger finger. "Look at your world. Everyone else is controlled by algorithms, but you here in this quaint little town are not. Why should you escape the control of artificial intelligence? Societies have been losing their social skills for decades, yet you communicate on a deeper level away from our gaze. Your worth is supposed to be tailored for economic benefit. You're too human. You're supposed to belong to us!"

Someone screamed. A gamer had shot a patron, turning her to ash. Another shriek occurred as the person still wrapped by an android's cable arm was crushed to death. The sharp snap of his ribs sounded like a dog crunching a bone. I was pulled out of the door by Carter. I was still holding onto Sage.

We dodged deathly rays as more gamers shot at us, protecting their androids from our defenceless selves. The front door of the pub burned, yet some braved the flames to escape the carnage. We ran from the cries for help. I tried to block them out. I wanted to get far enough away to fool myself none of this was happening.

I kept Sage and Carter in view. They often looked back to check I was keeping up.

"Where are we going?" Sage yelled.

"Just run," Carter screamed.

Another two helicopters flew by.

Parts of Cradle Edge I'd never seen whisked past. Attractive brick houses. Large green parks. A restaurant strip.

My badly timed sightseeing was another way to block out the reality of our situation. But of course, it didn't work.

I stopped, puffing to catch my breath. Sage bolted back and clutched my arm, urging me on. I continued, gathering pace. Fear motivated me. Fear of losing my organic self to artificial intelligence. Fear of being forced to have sex with Cambridge. Fear of a world without Sage.

I don't remember how long we'd been running before we noted there were no others escaping with us. Around us, ordinary citizens were oblivious to the danger of androids and their mind-controlled gamers.

A café full of diners enjoyed what might be their last meal. Barbers cut hair for clients who wouldn't have worried about personal appearance if they knew what was coming. And a toddler played with a go-cart in a park as her mother watched.

Carter ran into the café. "Everyone, leave!" he shouted. "You're all in danger." The customers glared at him as if he was mad.

I rushed into the barber shop, instructing them to do the same. "There are killer androids coming for you." I felt stupid as they laughed at what I'd said.

We heard the helicopters before we saw them fly past. Fast-paced steps were also audible.

"Everyone, leave!" Carter yelled again. "Now!"

"You're all in danger," I shouted.

The diners bolted first, followed by the staff. When the barbers and their customers saw the others rush in terror, they quickly followed.

Several choppers landed, but we hid ourselves in the horde, scurrying for our lives. When another helicopter flew past, people ran in different directions. We scampered with a team of ten others, believing that one of them knew which way was safest. One guy ran in his pyjamas.

A grey-haired woman lagged behind. Carter kept stopping to check on her, encouraging her to not give up. Sage and I took turns carrying the toddler, keeping her mother from being weighed down.

I thought about Sage and how lucky I was to find him. I loved his hard-edged personality. I wondered what living with him would be like. This contemplation was my distraction.

We finally made some distance between us and the attackers.

"Look!" Carter pointed.

An empty cargo ship was docked. A man with a hard hat and an orange vest was urging everyone to get on. People jumped on board.

"What if he's—" I tried to say.

"He can't be," Carter assured me.

"How do you know?" Sage asked.

"There's no internet out at sea. At least not at Cradle Edge because..." Carter knew his argument was redundant.

"You know there is. Cambridge and Audrey were powered by Social Media Central." Sage bowed his head.

"The infrastructure is obviously here." I gazed at the boat. "We need to take that chance. The internet can't be as strong at sea as it is on land."

"How can you be sure, man?" Sage grinned, knowing it was our only hope.

CHAPTER TWENTY-NINE

"WE ARE AUSTRALIAN refugees leaving the promised land in droves." I felt the night chill.

Sage and I sat on the rusted deck. I pressed my back against him as he wrapped his arms around my chest. His cheek met mine. Carter was elsewhere on the ship.

The sky teemed with stars. A million galaxies gazing back at us from the past. Countless ecosystems as mysterious as our own. And in that vastness, there were probably civilisations that would never be stupid enough to let artificial intelligence take over.

"You know, Sage, a few days ago I met a robot that made sarcastic comments about my personality. He hardly knew me yet analysed everything about me on Social Media Central. And he was witty! And hours ago, an android was flirting with me. I know so many people back in Astra City whose thought patterns are nowhere near as sophisticated."

"Judging by the diary Lilly-Of-The-Valley read, I think we've been dumbed down. My Enemy Alien playmates were definitely dumbed down."

"I think there was a time artificial intelligence couldn't match the depth of human emotion. Or complex thought. Or deep discussion. So, they had to dumb us down through our devices to a level artificial intelligence could understand. Eventually, they kept us away from normal social experiences. Which is what I used to love about Cradle Edge, and Carter's Life Experience Mob encounters. Normal social interaction. Something to value when many have lost the art."

"Man, it's not healthy to obsess over this."

"I can't help it." I gazed into his eyes. "Think about it. Every android we've seen is more human than the last. That means long before we were toilet trained, the plan to replace what makes us human for a system that guides our thoughts was being planned."

"You're still obsessing over it."

"I know, but it's freaky when you think about it. Societies guided by the human condition are irrelevant to those in power. Possibly to those who once wanted to sell us their products. And the machines they built to conform us have taken over."

"I wonder what sex with Cambridge would be like?" Sage sounded keen to lighten the mood.

"Dangerous, I reckon. Even I wondered what bionic sex was like after I touched his lifelike skin. He poked me when he arrived." I lifted my shirt. The bruise on my chest was tender. "But I couldn't imagine him forcing his you-know-what up you-know-where."

"Jackhammer." Sage smirked. "But if his skin is that smooth, topping him would be okay."

"Only if he's a starfish. He'd snap it right off if he's a power-bottom." I turned to face my boyfriend. "Speaking of sex, I'll never find out what Edelweiss means. I'm sure it's something dirty."

Sage shook his head. "I'm sure it's not." He paused, taking in a deep breath of sea air. "Where do you think we're going?"

"Wherever there's a pocket, a country, a county, shit, I don't know. Wherever the World Bank hasn't made us the machines, and androids aren't run on Social Media Central and blah blah blah..."

"You're tired."

"Yes. I'm not sleepy. I'm just sick and tired of the times we live in."

My head now rested against his chest. I closed my eyes to block out the murmurs of the many on board. It was time to escape into Sage Land. His beating heart was my lullaby.

"Man, I guess this solves the problem of whether to live in Astra City or stay at Cradle Edge." He laughed.

I'd heard him chuckle before, but this was a hearty laugh. The laugh of a man comfortable in his own skin. The laugh of someone who didn't care what others thought. A lot had happened to the person I met who once eyed me with caution. And he let me know it, sparring with me in that motel room.

"What would be your perfect life?" I mumbled into his chest.

"Us, together, of course."

"Where?" I sat up.

"A town. I'm over cities. I want a house big enough to wander in. To see the ocean from our bedroom window."

"You'll get sick of the ocean in a few days if we don't dock."

"The ocean. A cliff. I don't care. I want to see stars, man. I want a view where no one can see us screw any time of day."

"And no internet."

"And no internet."

I kissed him, lingering in that lovers' space where only *we* existed. And while our lips had met many times, this was yet another moment I knew he was my future. There was no longer an independent Tayler. I'd entered a new realm. One where home was the sensation of being in his arms.

"I want a dog," he said.

"A dog?"

"We'll need someone to bitch about each other to, and a dog will never tell you what I said." Sage peered down his nose at me. "Why are you laughing?"

"I was in a romantic headspace before you said that. But that's what I like about you. You bring me back to reality."

"Promise me something, Tayler."

"What, *man*?"

"Stop me from doing that. You need to keep dreaming while awake."

"You know me too well."

Starlight does wonders for the skin. Sage's face shone as if an accomplished make-up artist just prepared him for his cameo in a web series. My favourite co-star, or in this moment, my leading man.

"I like you when you're in this romantic headspace," he said.

"I've stopped obsessing and making the most of our time-out from gun-slinging gamers and their executioner androids. This is one of those moments I need to dream while awake."

"I know." His smile sunk into his cheeks.

"You escaped!" The old man with the sculptured hair spotted us. He ambled our way. "Where's the other guy and girl?"

"Carter's somewhere on the ship." I looked towards the opposite end. "As for Hudson, we don't know. We were supposed to catch up with her until the robots got nasty."

"I'm Jack." He offered his hand. We shook it, introducing ourselves. "Those damn robots! Where did they come from?"

"Some wild place," I replied. "They've got it in for the human race, yet they need us. They need us to be subservient."

"Were they made by man or by other robots?" Jack searched my face as if I could answer.

"What do you think?" Sage replied.

Jack shook his head.

"They're killing machines," I said. "Sophisticated anti-human killing machines."

"Tayler, go back to dreaming." Sage caressed my back.

"I should leave you alone," Jack said.

"No, stay," Sage replied. "Give us hope." He stared out to sea. "Tell me what we'll do when we get to wherever we're going."

"Wherever that is, I want a dog." Jack replied.

"See, Tayler. Everyone needs a dog."

"Another mouth to feed when we grow our own food." Regardless of my comment, I pictured a playful Jack Russell.

"I want to live alone," Jack said. "No internet, but I want a laptop for creative stuff. And an apartment with good people living around me. Dinner parties at my place with my neighbours. Brunch at theirs. Maybe I'll meet the woman of my dreams next door."

"I want a house," I said. "I want a view from our bedroom. I want to wake up, look at the view while reading that thing they used to publish in the past. There must be a small town where someone publishes those things."

"A book?" Jack asked.

"Close. Black text, colour photos, big sheets of paper."

"A newspaper." Jack replied.

"Yep. That's it! Something I can read to make up my own mind about the world. And I want to have a shop or a hobby—"

"Like growing your own food to feed our dog," Sage interrupted.

"Something. Anything that will make me connect with people. I know! A theatre group. We'll put on plays for the locals. Will you be my leading man, Sage?"

"Are you sure you don't want to be left alone?" Jack asked.

Sage smirked. "I used to be a serious gamer. This one..." He tickled me. "This one showed me how to connect. Hell, I need to connect." He eased my back into his chest again. "What did you do in Cradle Edge, Jack?"

"Hide."

I leaned forward. "Hide? From what?"

"From the World Bank. From a man named Stuart Manning. From the powers-that-be with inhuman plans." Jack studied my face. "What did I say?"

"Stuart Manning," Sage replied.

"You knew him?" I asked.

Jack nodded. "He bought Social Media Central from me."

"You *owned* Social Media Central?" I choked on my words.

"I created Social Media Central."

"Why?" Sage asked.

"I didn't create what it became." Jack shook his head vehemently. "No. No. No. I created it because different social media platforms courted different sections of society. Different ideologies weren't being contained by borders anymore. They were being amplified by different social media companies. The person next door had his own reality while the person down the street had another. Then I created something which was central. All the self-made illiterates only looking at pictures were forced to start reading again. While the nice family next door types were believing anything fed into their feed and voted accordingly. There was not one source for editorial truth where everyone was on the same page."

"Sounds kind of familiar." I thought back to the diary Lilly retold.

"Thus I created a social media platform to absorb them all, breaking down those ideologies with fact checks on anything anyone posted. A central place where everyone came together, which was what social media was originally designed for. Until Stuart Manning made it into something different."

Jack grinned at me. "Tayler, I recognised you at the pub. I was in Astra City when you were a social influencer. I knew Stuart was behind the rise of Connor, Shaun, and Madeline Q, but when you showed up, you were the unlikely hero of the group."

"Were you a fan of mine?"

"Not a fan. I was fascinated with what Stuart did with my software and how you ended up in the mix. I mean, Social Media Central was my baby. I was horrified and intrigued by what he'd done."

"He's dead now." My deadpan tone even surprised me.

"What!"

"A robot ordered his execution," I continued. "I was there."

Jack turned away, lost in his own thoughts. Sage and I stayed silent.

On the deck, some considered sleeping. One mother sang to her child. Others listened to the ocean, finding their own serenity. A few snored gently. The dreamers meditated out to sea. And Carter appeared, stepping cautiously over slumbering bodies to reach us.

"This is Jack," Sage said. "This is Carter."

Carter handed me his device while he and Jack shook hands. I glanced at the screen. Hudson had sent a message.

Tell Tayler Edelweiss is a song from a movie that's a hundred years old about a singing nun. Vanessa and I sing it whenever we're drunk together. Tell Tayler it has no exotic meaning at all because that's what he's thinking.

Also, I didn't find my vaper but I'm safe. Look after yourselves. Love, H.

"Satisfied?" Carter asked. "She sent it hours ago when we were running. It's proof Social Media Central is operating in my home town."

"Edelweiss is from a movie?" I shrugged. "And it's a song sung by singing nuns? Nah. That can't be right. I'm sure it's something kinky."

Sage poked my ribs. "Jack invented Social Media Central," he told Carter.

Carter stared at our new friend as if he was about to grow fangs, sprout hair, and howl at the moon.

"He invented it for good, not evil," Sage explained. "He invented it to bring people together."

"Away from different social media platform ideologies." I sounded enthusiastic even though I wasn't.

"Imagine what it could have been," said Carter.

"It would never have been." Sage didn't sound like he was addressing us. "Humans, man. Humans would still fuck it up."

"There's still good in the dream of social media," Jack said. "Human connection. Conversation. The chance to reach out and hear another point of view."

"That's what it was once." Carter squeezed in next to me and Sage.

"Another history lesson," I said.

"What do you mean?" Carter asked.

"Nothing," I replied. "It's just that the motel owner told

us the same thing."

"I want to hear Carter's version," Sage said. "I was stoned when I heard Lilly's."

"We studied it in university," Carter replied. "People initially debated, respectful of each other. They saw posts and comments in real time, not through some algorithm that picked whose posts you saw. So different points of view came through their feeds all the time. The same way a society worked. Different points of view sparking conversation every hour, every day." He took his device from his pocket and gazed at its screen. "Until this was merely a mirror of what someone believed. The social media companies fed back what its user already thought was true."

"That's where the stupid people come in," Sage said proudly. "Dumb peeps connected, amplifying misinformation and attacking the people who thought things through." Carter stared at Sage like he'd discovered a child-genius. "Maybe I wasn't as stoned as I thought. Lilly said this."

"That's what went wrong," Jack said. "The mistrust of facts and those who presented them. Journalists. Scientists."

"And when the media lost its teeth and didn't hold people to account for misinforming..." Carter shrugged. "Or media companies attacked each other because their particular audience had a different ideology..."

"Do you mean different media companies catered to their audiences and filtered out the news they should have shared for fear they'd lose that audience?" I gazed at the ocean. "That's what I read from the Alta Net. And what I heard from Lilly. Some media empires lost their teeth when they should have let their audience know certain facts. And the masses came with pitchforks for those who weren't hoodwinked by things that didn't make sense."

"And those who weren't hoodwinked didn't see it coming," Jack continued. "Those who weren't hoodwinked still saw the world the way the generation before taught them. They knew science mattered. They knew a politician was as good as his actions, not his media spin. They knew it was cruel to lock away those affected by political wargames then convince society to demonise them."

"The hoodwinked were rewired." My words drifted out to sea. "Their morals replaced with fear of things that didn't matter, and blindness to the effect this had."

"Lilly's words sunk in," Sage said to me.

"Lilly's words and other stuff," I replied.

We all gazed at the expanse. The deep blue sky. The endless ocean. A universe that felt infinitely safer than our own planet.

Chaos reigned in the country I was born, and there was no guarantee our ship of two hundred or so misplaced souls would find peace. We could be endless travellers finding mechanised madness wherever we docked. Or maybe out there, somewhere, was a forest or shoreline where we'd start again. Renew society with the lessons we'd learned. Give in to the elements Mother Nature always intended to share with us.

But I didn't have the energy to start anew.

Sage held my chin and examined my troubled face. He gave me a peck on the cheek. I kissed him as I needed his lips against mine. And somewhere in his embrace I recharged.

The last decades of the twenty-first century beckoned, and together with the man I loved, we'd reassess, or redefine, what it meant to be human.

This wasn't *my* wish. It was a moral necessity.

Acknowledgements

Writing a novel is a solitary endeavour, until it's ready for others to take the reins and make it better.

So, the first person to thank in making this book better is my editor, Elizabeth Coldwell. As always, you've found my mistakes and my Yoda-isms and fixed them for me.

Next, Raevyn McCann for providing a space for many of us to be heard.

Jaycee DeLorenzo, for visualising my work and creating a knock-out cover.

To Robin Hofmann for keeping check on Tayler's desires.

To Richard Platt, for learning lines, rehearsing, and playing Tayler again for the book trailer. You're great to work with.

And finally, to Brett Tyler, for not only giving me a studio to shoot a trailer, but also for helping direct and for mixing visual effects. I still have the pen you gave me as a gift at the start of my writing journey, all those years ago.

ABOUT KEVIN KLEHR

Kevin lives with his husband, Warren, in their humble apartment (affectionately named Sabrina), in Australia's own "Emerald City," Sydney.

His tall tales explore unrequited love in the theatre district of the Afterlife, romance between a dreamer and a realist, and a dystopian city addicted to social media.

His first novel, *Drama Queens with Love Scenes*, spawned a secondary character named Guy. Many readers argue that Guy, the insecure gay angel, is the star of the Actors and Angels book series. His popularity surprised the author.

The third in this series, *Drama Queens and Devilish Schemes*, scored a Rainbow Award (judged by fans of queer fiction) for Best Gay Alternative Universe/Reality novel.

More recently, his book, *The Midnight Man*, scored Runner Up in Best Gay Fantasy at the Rainbow Awards, while *Winter Masquerade* received an Honourable Mention. *The Midnight Man* also scored first place in an LGBT category at the Paranormal Romance Guild's Reviewers Choice Awards and won in the Fantasy category of the 2021 Gay Scribe Awards.

So, with Guy, his fictional guardian angel guiding him, Kevin hopes to bring more whimsical tales of love, life, and friendship to his readers.

Facebook:
www.facebook.com/DramaQueensWithLoveScenes

Twitter:
@kevinklehr

Instagram:
www.instagram.com/klehrkevin

YouTube:
www.youtube.com/user/KevinKlehr

Website:
www.kevinklehr.com

OTHER NINESTAR BOOKS BY THIS AUTHOR

Actors and Angels series
Drama Queens with Love Scenes
Drama Queens and Adult Themes
Drama Queens and Devilish Schemes

Nate and Cameron series
Nate and the New Yorker
Nate's Last Tango
The Nate and Cameron Collection

TAYLeR series
Social Media Central

Midnight Angel
From Top to Bottom
Winter Masquerade
The Midnight Man